THE MARRIAGE DIARIES

ERIKA WILDE

THE BEGINNING

a diary entry from Jillian Noble:

I love my husband. My sexy, alpha, ex-Navy SEAL. He still does it for me, but after nineteen years of marriage, our sex life has become routine. Some might call it vanilla. With our sons grown and out of the house, I'm ready to reinvent our relationship. I want more than ordinary sex. I'm ready to explore the forbidden and erotic, with a little kink and no more holding back.

Now, if I can convince my husband to give in to his own dark desires, all my fantasies will come true.

THE OFFICE VISIT

"*C*ome on, Jill, you can do it. It's not as though you've never seduced your husband before."

Sitting in her parked car, Jillian Noble exhaled a deep breath and waited for her encouraging pep talk to take effect and ease her nerves. Biting absently on her bottom lip, she stared up at the glass and chrome building where her husband's security consulting firm, Noble & Associates, resided on the twenty-eighth floor of the San Diego building. It was nearly two in the afternoon, and with Dean's silver Aston Martin Vantage coupe tucked neatly into his reserved spot, she knew he was in his office.

Now, it was just a matter of her gathering up the courage to saunter into Dean's domain and show her husband of nearly twenty years that she wanted to shake up their sex life.

At the age of thirty-eight, as well as being an ex-Navy SEAL who regularly trained with the men he hired to work for his security firm, Dean was still a gorgeous, virile man who enjoyed sex just as much as she did. But years of her focusing on raising their two sons along with being a wife and mother, and Dean working crazy long hours to ensure his security company was a success, well, the intimacy between them had become too predictable and routine. Somewhere along the way, they'd lost the intensity, the excitement and spontaneity, and she wanted all that back again… and much, much more.

Now that both boys were away—one in college and one enlisted in the Navy—and it was just her and Dean, she was ready to make the two of them a priority and revive their sex life in a major way, and take them both places they'd never dared to go before. Dark, erotic places she instinctively knew her husband had shied away from because he feared there was a part of his abusive father lurking deep inside him, and his biggest fear had always been that he'd go too far and hurt her.

With all her heart and soul, Jill knew her husband would never physically harm her, despite his own doubts. He'd never, ever, laid a hand on either of their two boys, not even when she, herself, wanted to strangle one of them for their idiotic teenage antics. Instead, Dean had taken the quiet and direct approach in disciplining their sons—starting with a strict discussion about right and wrong, and then he'd doled out their punishment, which usually included some kind of hard labor that gave them plenty of time to think about the stupidity of their actions.

Simple, but always effective.

A small smile curved the corner of her mouth. She'd be lying if she didn't admit that Dean could absolutely be over-bearing, possessive, and a bit controlling at times, but in their nineteen years of marriage, he'd never given her a reason not to trust him, in all ways.

Today would be the defining factor in their marriage. In the past, just as things got interesting in the bedroom, he'd pull back and gentle his touch and soften his words. The romance of making love had its place, but she wanted the raw, primitive man she knew Dean could be. And if it took a bit of coaxing to get him to release that staunch control of his and let go of all those fears holding him back, well, she figured she might as well have fun giving it her best shot.

Exhaling a deep breath, she stepped out of her Chevy Suburban and headed toward the building, her four inch black stilettos clicking on the paved walkway, then the marbled floors inside the lobby. Reaching the elevators, she stepped inside and punched the button for the twenty-eight floor.

On the flight up, she battled the nerves fluttering in her belly, the ones that made her question her sanity for going through with her outrageous plan. But then the double doors *whooshed* opened and Gail, the firm's long-time secretary, glanced up and greeted her with a genuine smile.

Now that Jill had been seen and recognized, there was no backing out now, so she walked into the plush reception area and stopped at the older woman's desk.

"Good afternoon, Jill," the other woman said, as warm and welcoming as always.

Jill smiled and tried to act casual, even though she was feeling anything but calm inside. "Hi, Gail. I'm here to see Dean. Is he available?"

"Absolutely. He's in his office." Gail reached for the phone on her desk. "Would you like for me to let him know you're here?"

"No, I'd rather surprise him," Jill said, stopping Gail before she could announce her presence and she lost the element of throwing her husband a little off kilter. Gaining the upper hand in any situation didn't happen often with Dean, and this was one time it would definitely work to her advantage.

"I'm sure he'd like that." Gail waved a hand toward the back offices, giving Jill the silent go-ahead.

She walked past Gail's desk, belatedly realizing just how close the secretary was to the other offices. Just behind the reception area was a large conference room, and she recognized the deep male voice talking as Dean's partner, Brent "Mac" MacMillan.

She glanced surreptitiously inside as she

passed and saw the back of Mac's broad shoulders, and three other big, buff, good-looking men who worked security detail for the company. They were standing straight in a row with their feet braced apart and hands clasped behind their backs in a stance she recognized as military trained.

Because Mac commanded their attention as he issued instructions for their next security detail, none of the three men acknowledged her, though their intuitive gazes definitely tracked her progress as she strolled by. The men Dean and Mac hired were all ex-military —tough, bad-ass, alpha men like her husband. Silent, always aware, and incredibly intense. Only the absolute best of the best for Noble and Associates.

She continued on her way. To the right was Mac's currently empty office, and to the left was her husband's. His door was halfway closed, and she knocked on the wooden surface before slipping inside and making an appearance.

He glanced up from the paperwork he'd been perusing, his dark, sable brows still furrowed in concentration. As soon as he saw her, his gray eyes flickered with surprise, then quickly shifted to concern. Because she knew him so well, she caught the subtle tensing of his body, that vigilant awareness that something was off.

"Hey, baby," he said, his calm tone belying just how alert he was. "Is everything okay?"

"Everything is just fine," she rushed to reassure him, before his over-protective demeanor took over and derailed her plans. She understood his worry—she didn't stop by the office often, and never without calling him first. Of course he'd think the worst.

She closed the door and pressed in the lock to assure them privacy, which didn't escape his notice. Knowing the rest of her plan succeeding now relied on Dean's response to what she did next, she bolstered her confidence one last time and slowly strolled toward him.

She put an extra sway in her hips, and tugged loose the tie on her wrap-around dress. She allowed the fabric to flutter open in front, just enough to tantalize him with a smooth expanse of thigh as she walked. Predictably, his gaze immediately dropped to the flash of skin, and the last of her nerves gave way to anticipation.

"I want to get your opinion on something I bought today," she said huskily.

He never cared about what she purchased for herself, but then again, she rarely spent frivolously or excessively, even when he encouraged her to spoil herself. They were well-off now, his company worth millions, but when they'd first married right out of high school with a baby on the way, saving and budgeting had become a habit for her—one she was just learning to break every once in a while. After today, she hoped to have a reason to continue to splurge.

"I went to Sugar and Spice today to visit Raina, and I found something I thought you might like, but I wanted to be absolutely sure." One of her good friends, Raina Beck, owned Sugar and Spice, an adult boutique that carried gorgeous lingerie, high end sex toys, and other erotic novelty items.

Dean was well aware of that, too.

He leaned back in his leather chair, regarding her with undisguised interest and a whole lot of heat in his eyes. "You definitely have my attention," he drawled in that low, sexy timbre that still had the ability to make her shiver like the infatuated girl she'd once been with him. Still was, actually.

She came around the side of his desk and stopped a few feet away, then released the belt on her dress, which opened completely. A shrug of her shoulders, and the material slid down both of her arms and pooled around her black stiletto heels, leaving her clad in nothing more than a push-up bra with just enough lace to cover her hardened nipples, and matching G-string panties—both in red, his favorite color on her.

She heard the breath rush from his lungs as he took in her skimpy, barely there attire. "Jesus, Jill," he said, his voice sounding shocked and strangled, though his intense, molten gray eyes glowed with appreciation.

Her stomach tumbled with desire. Her figure wasn't model perfect and she no longer possessed a young, nubile body. She'd given birth to two kids and while she watched her weight and did yoga five times a week, she had full breasts and curves that were soft and supple and womanly. And right now, with him devouring her with his gaze, she felt sexy and incredibly exhilarated.

She skimmed her fingers along the lace edge of her bra, then trailed them down her belly to the thin band of her panties. "Do you like it?" she asked oh-so-guilelessly.

"Hell, yeah, I like it," he growled deep in his throat. "A lot."

He'd yet to touch her, and that's what she wanted most of all. He was watching her as if he wasn't certain what to expect because this was so out of character for her, so she didn't hesitate to show him. Stepping between his spread knees, she braced one hand on the armrest so she was leaning over him, grabbed his deep purple tie with her other hand and pulled his mouth closer to hers.

"Good," she breathed against his lips. "Because I bought it with you in mind."

She slid her mouth against his, feeling his initial surprise, which thankfully didn't last long. With a groan that sounded like the sweetest of surrender, he buried his fingers into her hair and did what he did best... he took control of the situation.

His mouth claimed hers, firm and insistent,

his tongue hot and demanding as he deepened the kiss. She moaned softly, resisting the urge to crawl onto his lap and let him have his way with her, which he no doubt expected, because she always let him lead and bent to his will.

Not that having Dean in charge was a bad thing, but today was all about switching things up, being adventurous and spontaneous, and showing him she wanted *more* sexually. That she was open to a whole lot more than sex in the bedroom, and there were fantasies she wouldn't mind fulfilling with him.

She kissed him back just as passionately, feeling the hunger growing in him, the molten need... and then, abruptly, he grasped her hair tighter and pulled her head back, ending the kiss. Breathing hard, he stared into her eyes, looking dazed, a little confused, and excruciatingly aroused by her bold and brazen behavior.

"Jillian... what the hell are you doing?"

His voice was soft and dangerous, a subtle warning that he was on edge. Clearly, he was fighting the urge to give in to the lust burning in his gaze because they were in his office, with co-workers just beyond the closed door.

Yeah, she'd definitely thrown him off balance, and she liked having that advantage.

"I'm seducing you," she said, and gave him an equally alluring smile. "Is it working yet?"

He took the hand she'd braced on the chair and flattened her palm against the hard length of his erection bulging the front of his slacks. "What do *you* think?"

"Oh." Her eyes widened in feigned innocence, and she gave his thick shaft a firm squeeze. "I didn't mean to get you so hot and bothered."

He raised a dark brow, amusement and daring etching his ruggedly handsome features. "Now that you have, what are you going to do about it?"

His gruff demand sent swirls of sexual heat spiraling straight down to her stomach. This was what Jill wanted, for Dean to play along and allow the fantasy to unfold into hot, tantalizing reality. She let her lashes fall half-mast and licked her bottom lip, summoning the words she'd never, ever, said to him before. "I'm going to suck your cock and make you come."

Dean's mouth opened, then snapped shut

again, his jaw tense. Her husband was rarely at a loss for words, but her candid, explicit reply rendered him shocked and speechless. The slow burn of excitement in his eyes, however, assured her that he was fascinated by her brazen transformation.

Thoroughly enjoying her newfound power, she knelt between his spread legs and began unbuckling his belt, anxious to make good on her promise. He watched her through hooded eyes, his breathing deepening as she unbuttoned his slacks, opened the zipper, then tugged his pants and boxer briefs low on his hips so that his fierce erection sprang free.

Knowing he still needed to be presentable for the rest of the day, she pushed the hem of his shirt up to his chest and out of her way, and couldn't resist the urge to lean forward and place a hot, wet, open-mouthed kiss against the taut muscles just below his navel.

"Oh, fuck…" he rasped, like a man on the verge of insanity.

Smiling to herself, she trailed her damp lips lower. The intoxicating masculine scent of him aroused her, and the taste of him—all hot, hard male—saturated her senses and made her insides clench with need.

Gripping his shaft firmly in one hand, she wrapped her lips around the swollen crown of his dick, taking him into her mouth just a few excruciating inches. She swirled her tongue along the tip, then took him deep, until her lips touched the base of his cock and the sensitive head rubbed enticingly against the back of her throat. She swallowed, wrenching a groan of pure ecstasy from him.

She slid him in and out of her mouth, stroking him with her tongue and adding just enough suction to keep him on edge. His hand cupped the back of her head, but he didn't push or thrust into her mouth the way she knew he instinctively wanted to, the way *she* wanted him to. Didn't grip her hair tight and use a little force to make her give him what he needed the most. He held back, always in control, when she was dying for him to dominate her and take whatever pleasure he desired the most.

Another time, she promised herself. For now, she made his orgasm her ultimate goal. She continued blowing him, increasing the friction of her fingers along the hard column of

ERIKA WILDE

flesh, and deepening the wet suction of her mouth as she doubled her efforts to make him come. His entire body tensed, and he gasped a warning, tightening his fingers in her hair to pull her head away.

She refused to release him. His hips jerked wildly, and she felt the tell-tale pulsing of his cock in her mouth give way to a surge of warmth that she didn't hesitate to swallow. With a hum of feminine power and delight, she finished him off, until she'd wrung him dry and he sagged back against his leather chair, dazed and temporarily wasted.

She remained kneeling in front of Dean, back arched slightly, hands resting on her thighs, waiting patiently for him to recover, because she wasn't done seducing him just yet. He glanced down at her, and she watched as his gaze darkened as he took in her very subdued, obedient-like pose, something she suspected would rouse him all over again.

Oh, yeah, he liked her subservient demeanor. A lot. They'd never played at being dominant/submissive, but there had been enough instances in the bedroom when he'd displayed just enough aggression to give her the indication that he was on the cusp of tipping over into a more authoritative role sexually, yet was denying his true nature and had been for years.

But exploring those D/s themes was for another day, another time, when they weren't confined to his office with the possibility of being interrupted.

Still wearing her red lacy bra, G-string, and fuck-me stilettos, she rose to her feet and leisurely skimmed her hands down her stomach, smiling to herself as his sinful gaze tracked the direction her fingers were heading... right into the waistband of her panties.

"I have another surprise for you," she said huskily.

"I don't know that I can handle another surprise," he said, though he hadn't looked away from where her fingers had disappeared.

She laughed softly. "Oh, I think you can."

Hooking her thumbs into the thin strings at the sides of her hips, she pushed her panties down and let them fall away, revealing her freshly waxed mound.

He groaned his appreciation, and she teased him a bit more, grazing the tips of her fingers along the smooth, newly naked flesh. He'd always wanted her to go completely bare, and she'd never had the nerve. But she had to admit that getting a full Brazilian wax had been quite liberating.

He flashed her one of his patented bad boy grins... the same one she'd fallen hard and fast for back in high school. The same one that still had the ability to make her weak in the knees now.

"If I didn't know better, I'd think today was my birthday."

She tipped her head to the side, letting her long dark hair tumble sexily over her shoulder. "Would you like to see... everything?" she teased.

"*Hell, yeah*," he said without hesitation. "Sit on my desk, spread your legs, and show me."

His demand ramped up her own excitement. Pushing aside the papers and files he'd been perusing when she'd arrived, she lifted herself up onto his desk, so that her legs were dangling. But she didn't give him the view he'd asked for... not just yet. He was still sprawled in his leather chair, much too far away, his body deceptively lax.

She crooked her finger at her husband. "Come closer. You're too far away and I want to make sure you get a *very* good look."

"You're fucking killing me," he muttered, though there was unmistakable humor in his voice as he rolled his chair closer.

Before she could open her legs, he wrapped his long, strong fingers around one of her ankles and placed the stiletto heel on the leather armrest of his chair, then did the same to her other leg, spreading her indecently, shamelessly wide.

"Do *not* move your feet," he ordered as he sat up in his chair, which brought him intimately close to the crux of her thighs. "Lean back on your arms so I can see every smooth, waxed inch of you."

She did as he asked, bracing herself on her forearms and exposing herself even more to him.

His nostrils flared, and his eyes blazed with lust as he looked his fill. "That is so fucking hot," he said as he slowly traced a finger along the lips of her sex, which were now hypersensitive to his touch. "You have such a gorgeous cunt."

His coarse words, spoken so reverently, thrilled her, made her feel giddy with the knowledge that he liked what he saw.

His fingers dipped into her core and spread the slick moisture along the folds of flesh, all the way up to her aching clit, stroking her slowly, expertly. She bit her bottom lip as her thighs began to quiver, while he glanced up at her face, taking in the thick fall of her hair, then the swell of her breasts nearly spilling from the scrap of lace barely covering them.

"You're so soft, so smooth, and very, very wet." He pushed two fingers back inside her body, sliding his thumb against that sensitive nub of flesh once again, teasing and tormenting her.

"Sucking you off does that to me," she managed to reply, and it was the absolute truth.

"I think I need to return the favor," he said, and moved even closer. He draped her legs over his broad shoulders, then dipped his head and trailed moist, suckling kisses up the inside of her thigh.

Watching him go down on her was so decadent and erotic, how he closed his eyes as he nuzzled his way toward her pussy, the way he blew a hot gust of air on her wet folds, and that first leisurely lick of his tongue that made her body jolt in shock before he settled his mouth completely over her and sucked her clit.

The surprising scrape of his teeth added another dimension of delightful bliss. She moaned out loud as pleasure, fast and fierce, lashed through her. Unable to support herself any longer, she laid back on his desk, her back arching off the surface as his tongue continued to flick and swirl and his long fingers pumped deep inside her, heightening the searing, relentless sensory assault.

Her body tingled with needs so intense she felt as though she was going to explode. And then she did. Her hips bucked against his tenacious mouth as her orgasm crashed through her, stealing her breath for a moment before releasing it in a soft, keening cry. Tremors quaked through her, one after the other, and she rode the wave for as long as it lasted.

Her climax had literally left her reeling, and she was vaguely aware of Dean lurching to his feet. Wrapping his strong arms around her thighs, he hauled her bottom to the very edge of his desk, then slammed into her with such shocking force she felt as though her world had tipped on its axis.

She sucked in a startled gasp as he began to thrust, impaling her hard and incredibly deep. Each rapid plunge of his hips shoved her higher and higher onto the desk, until she felt as though she was going to slide off the other side.

Eyes wide, her arms flew out to her sides to grab *something* to hold onto for the wild, unexpected ride, and ended up knocking over a photo frame and some kind of paperweight. Both landed on the floor with a loud thud and clatter—enough noise to draw attention from anyone outside the office.

She cringed, but Dean didn't stop moving. His arms banded around her thighs, keeping her legs wide open so he could watch as he pumped in and out of her in long, solid strokes. The man was very visual, and he liked to see *everything* as he fucked her.

The intercom on his phone beeped, followed by his secretary's concerned voice. "Is everything all right, Mr. Noble? I heard a loud noise and wanted to make sure everything is okay."

"Everything is fine, Gail," Dean replied in a surprisingly normal voice, even as he surged into Jill once again with a grinding motion of his hips that forced her to bite back a telltale moan. "My wife accidentally knocked a few things off my desk."

Jill's face flamed in mortification as he disconnected the call and smirked knowingly at her.

"You are so bad," she said, trying not to laugh.

He slowed the rhythm of his thrusts, as if wanting to savor the pleasure, his own gray eyes glimmering with humor as he met her gaze. "Would you have me any other way?"

"No," she replied honestly, because she wanted to see a whole lot more of this incorrigible bad boy who didn't hesitate to screw her in his office, with people right outside the door.

"I also didn't expect you to get hard again." She smirked right back at him, though she loved that she'd turned him on that much.

"That's what going down on *you* does to *me*." He licked his still damp lips, the lazy in and out of his shaft making her restless for

23

more. "I love the way you taste. Like ripe juicy peaches and cream. I could eat you for hours."

A full-bodied shiver coursed through her, and her inner walls clenched tighter around his shaft. The man certainly had a way with words.

"Show me your breasts," he murmured.

There wasn't a front clasp on her bra, so she lowered the straps down her arms until the panel of lace fell away. Knowing how much he liked watching her touch herself, she cupped both mounds of flesh in her hands and squeezed them together, then tugged on her nipples until they turned into hard pink pebbles. She rolled them between her fingers, and flicked the taut, sensitive tips with her thumbs. The quickening of his thrusts told her how much he enjoyed the show.

"What do *these* taste like?" she asked, her voice a sultry, playful purr.

"Like sweet cherries," he drawled huskily.

Reaching up to him, she slid her fingers into his silky hair and drew his mouth down to her breasts, the length of his strong, muscular body now pressing hers more firmly into the hard wooden desk. "Lick them."

He dipped his head and slid the flat of his

soft, velvety tongue over her aureole, then nipped at her with his teeth and sucked her into his mouth. The hot, wet sensation shot an arrow of desire straight down to where they joined, where his thrusts were picking up pace and becoming more insistent. More urgent.

She wrapped her legs around his hips and slid her hands beneath his shirt and up the slope of his spine, urging him on. With a low, feral growl, he lunged upward and kissed her, sealing their lips and buffering her soft moan of need.

His hot mouth devoured. His wicked tongue pillaged. Roughly, he shoved his hands through her hair, wrapping the long strands around his fingers, holding her captive as he ravaged her mouth with the same edgy, desperate way he took her body.

Deeper and deeper. Harder and faster.

Her fingernails dug into his muscled back as he plunged, again and again. Everything about him was hard and strong, all primitive, animalistic, carnal male. The incredible power of his passion sent another orgasm rippling through her body, and thank God he still had his mouth locked tight over hers or else her scream of pleasure would have undoubtedly been heard by all.

Dean was right behind her with his own release, a guttural groan vibrating from deep in his chest as his body jerked hard against hers. He collapsed on top of her, both of them breathing fast as they tried to calm their racing hearts.

In time, he lifted off her and straightened, his clothing as askew and rumpled as his hair. He helped her off his desk, picked up her discarded clothes from the floor, and handed them to her.

"Go ahead and use the bathroom to get dressed," he said, nodding his head toward the private quarters connected directly to his office.

She disappeared into the luxurious bathroom, decorated in sleek black tile and chrome accents. She cleaned up and put her panties and dress back on, then glanced in the mirror above the sink. Bright blue eyes, a few shades darker than her normal sky blue, stared back at her. Her lips were swollen from Dean's kisses, and her complexion was flushed with sated passion. She ran her fingers through her disheveled hair, incredibly pleased with the way her visit with her husband had played out. His response had been better than she'd imagined.

She stepped back into his office and found him sitting in his chair, all tucked in and zipped up. His hair was still ruffled from the way she'd clutched those thick strands in her hands just minutes before, and she loved that he wasn't like one of those prissy metro-sexual males who had soft, manicured hands and untouchable hair that was always in place. Dean was a man's man, rugged and alpha and secure in his masculinity, without any excess trappings. He was bold, confident, yet always a gentleman.

Those more gallant, honorable qualities had their time and place, but just as men preferred a lady in public and a whore in private, Jill had come to the conclusion that she wanted a rake and a libertine in the bedroom, and all of the down and dirty, risqué acts that came with her husband being an assertive, demanding lover. And in order to get what she desired, she had to ask for it. Demand it. Take it as her due as Dean's wife.

His gaze met hers, and while his body was relaxed, there was a slight crease between his brows that told her he was analyzing the situation, and her. It was difficult to tell what he was thinking, because he was good at hiding his feelings and emotions. She wanted that to change, too.

"Come here," he said, and held his hand out to her.

Placing her fingers in his warm palm, she let him pull her toward him and guide her so that she was sitting across his lap. He wrapped one arm around her waist and settled his other hand on her thigh, exposed by the opening slit of her dress. His touch was hot but gentle, as was the look in his eyes as he met her gaze.

"Care to tell me what that was all about?" he asked.

His tone was curious, and Jill knew this is where everything was about to change. That being open and honest with him would either make their relationship stronger, or break their marriage. Depending on how he viewed her bold request.

"I thought it was obvious," she said with a

flirty smile. "It was all about putting some spontaneity into our sex life."

He arched a dark brow. "You've never been impulsive."

True. She was more practical by nature, having been raised by conservative, wealthy parents who always had a plan for everything... including their daughter's future, which hadn't included Jillian getting pregnant at the age of seventeen by a defiant, rebellious boy from the very low income, and rough neighborhood on the outskirts of Austin, Texas. She'd been the quintessential good girl, until Dean and all his arrogance and swagger had coaxed her to take a walk on the wild side with him.

He'd been so mysterious and exciting, yet incredibly sweet and gentle with her, and it hadn't taken long for the two of them to fall in love. Even as a teenager, he'd faced his responsibilities like a man, including his commitment to her and their unborn child.

Though her parents had insisted Jillian put their baby up for adoption, she'd refused and married Dean on her eighteenth birthday at the local courthouse—just five days before he left for Navy basic training. And that's when she'd learned to finely hone those practical, sensible qualities, because she was now a wife and months later, a mother to a baby boy.

Their second son arrived fifteen months later, and with Dean serving an eight year term as a Navy SEAL, being impulsive was something that hadn't really fit into their lives for the past nineteen years.

Now it did.

"Having two grown boys always running around the house, along with their friends, made spontaneity difficult," she admitted. "But now that they're both gone, maybe it's time to shake things up... and try new things."

He frowned, and she could see the glimmer of concern in his gaze. "Are you unhappy?"

"With us, as a couple?" She shook her head adamantly and placed her palm against his jaw in reassurance, liking the slight stubble already forming there. "No. I love you, Dean. More now than ever."

The worry in his eyes ebbed, and she continued. "I just sometimes think that with us getting married at such a young age that you and I haven't been able to explore other things to enhance our sex life."

The corner of his mouth twitched, enough to tell Jillian that she'd captured his interest. "Define other things," he said.

"Being impulsive, like today in your office, instead of both of us crawling into bed at night, exhausted and doing the same old thing," she said, injecting a bit of teasing into her voice. "Making love with you is always amazing, but you have to admit it's become very... routine, and vanilla."

"Vanilla, huh?" There was no disagreement in his tone, just speculation of the word she'd used to describe their current sex life. "So, what would you call what just happened here in my office?"

She grinned. "A mocha hot fudge sundae with sprinkles and a cherry on top."

He chuckled and nuzzled her neck with his soft, damp lips. "The cherries were *especially* good."

She shivered in delight at his playfulness, and caught the hand that was skimming its way up her thigh, knowing if those skillful fingers reached their destination this conversation

ERIKA WILDE

would be over... and she wasn't ready for it to be over, not yet. When she walked out of his office, she wanted to know that they were both on the same page, and wanted the same thing.

"I'm being serious, Dean." Threading her fingers through his hair, she tugged his head back so he was looking into her eyes again. "I want to explore different things and push our sexual boundaries. Any fantasies we have, any toys we want to try, role playing, dirty talk, I'm open to it all."

"Do you want kink?"

He asked the question tentatively, as if the possibility interested him, but he didn't want to push something she wasn't willing to explore.

"Yes, I want kink." Because with him, a man she trusted unconditionally, she knew anything out of the ordinary would be erotic and excit- ing. "And I want you to stop holding back during sex."

She felt him tense, as if she'd caught him in some kind of lie. "What makes you think I am?"

"Because you're my husband and I know *you*. And I can feel it." Before he could deny her claim, she went on. "Sometimes, when things get a little rough, or interesting, you pull back

32

because you're afraid you're going to take things too far or hurt me. I can handle you being rough and dominant." In fact, the thought of being under his command excited her.

"What if you can't handle it?" The gruff bite to his voice belied his deeper concerns. The ones he feared the most.

"Then you have to trust me to tell you so," she replied gently, but firmly. "*You* need this, and want this, just as much as I do."

He didn't argue or deny the truth. Before she could say anything else, his intercom buzzed and Gail's voice drifted out. "Mr. Noble, your two o'clock appointment is here."

Dean glanced at the clock on the wall and swore beneath his breath. "Put Mr. Loren in the conference room, and let him know that I'll be there in a few minutes."

"Will do," Gail said, and disconnected the call.

"Shit." Dean scrubbed a hand along his jaw and gave Jillian a stern look. "You made me forget all about the meeting I had scheduled for this afternoon with a very important client."

She should have told him she was sorry, but

honestly, she wasn't the least bit contrite about seducing her husband. "Then I guess I should be going."

She stood up, and so did he. Just as she turned to walk around his desk, he grabbed her wrist and pulled her back around again. His heated gaze roamed over her disheveled hair, then her face, and he smirked that confident, cocky smile of his.

"You do realize, don't you, that you look like you've just been fucked."

She didn't miss the possessive inflection in his voice. Already, she sensed a change in him, a darker edge that excited her. "I feel like it, too," she said, unable to deny that she was very tender in the most delicious places. "Do you think anyone will notice that you had your way with me when I walk out of your office?"

"I'm sure they will."

And he wanted them to! The rogue.

He jerked her toward him, and she stumbled on her stilettos and fell against his unyielding chest with a gasp of surprise. His mouth came down on hers in a hard, deep, aggressive kiss that claimed, consumed, and branded her. The connection was sizzling hot, and brimming with erotic promise.

Just as abruptly as he'd kissed her, he let her go. "I'll see you at home later this evening."

There was a definite command in his words, as if he expected her to be waiting for him—which, of course, she would be. She'd taken a huge leap of faith with her husband today, revealing wants and desires that had been denied for too long. Now she just had to wait and see what hand Dean would play when he came home from work tonight.

BE CAREFUL WHAT YOU WISH FOR

*W*hile a pot of creamy beef stroganoff simmered on the stove for dinner, Jillian went about slicing and dicing vegetables for a salad, expecting Dean home any time, since he'd texted her a while ago to let her know he was leaving the office shortly. She always liked having a hot meal waiting for him, and he always seemed to appreciate the effort.

She loved to cook... especially in the gourmet kitchen Dean had insisted she have when they'd drawn up the specs for their custom built home. For the first fifteen years of their marriage they'd lived in middle income neighborhoods before finally being able to afford to build the house of their dreams. And while she'd never complained about their modest lifestyle and had learned to budget their money well during those leaner years, she knew that Dean had big goals, and that had included being a self-made man and being wealthy enough to give Jillian every luxury he thought she deserved.

Those were the things that drove him on a daily basis. It never mattered how much she assured him that she was happy, so long as she was with him and the boys—for Dean, he measured his success in what he could provide in material objects, because of his own impoverished childhood.

But what he didn't realize was that the things he'd given her that were most precious were not tangible items or valuable assets. She might have been raised by filthy rich parents who'd given her every advantage until she'd married Dean, but he'd provided unconditional love, security, and happiness. Emotional things that money could never buy. His strong work ethic had allowed her to be a stay-at-home wife and mother, and she loved taking care of her boys and Dean.

Making sure that they were happy made her feel complete.

Smiling to herself, she dumped the cubed tomatoes and cucumbers into the salad bowl, then turned to stir the pot of stroganoff when she caught sight of a male figure out of the corner of her eye. She gasped, even as she realized it was Dean who was leaning against the door jamb, startled by the fact that he'd managed to come into the house so silently.

Then again, the man was a trained SEAL, and the element of stealth and surprise was something they, and he, excelled in.

"Jesus, Dean," she said, exasperated, as she turned off the burner on the stove. "I didn't hear you come in from the garage and you startled me. When did you get home?"

"A few minutes ago."

And clearly he'd been quietly watching her, studying her. His stance was deceptively casual, contradicting the burning heat in his gaze as it raked over her, taking in the tank top and form fitting yoga pants she'd changed into after taking a shower a few hours ago. When his stormy gray eyes met hers again, he looked agitated and dear Lord, she felt... aroused.

She swallowed, uncertain of his true mood, yet sensing an undercurrent of change in the air, and that excited her, too. This restless, mercurial man was very different from the relaxed one she'd kissed good-bye this morning as he'd left for work, and she welcomed the transformation, and everything it implied.

"Is everything okay?" she asked. Clearly, it wasn't, and she was dying to know what was going through that sexy head of his.

"Hardly," he bit out, then pushed off the door frame and slowly strolled toward her, predatory like. "Do you realize how badly your visit today disrupted my entire afternoon?"

He didn't appear angry, but he was definitely perturbed. He continued his stalking approach, and she took a tentative step back, until her spine came into contact with the edge of the granite counter top and she couldn't retreat any further.

Did you not make it to your meeting?" she asked.

He stopped in front of her, braced his hands on either side of the counter so she was trapped between two very solid surfaces, and leaned in close. "I made it to the meeting just fine," he said gruffly. "But I couldn't think straight for shit, and Mac had to handle most of the contract details with the client because he clearly noticed I was... *off.*"

Dean was a man with extreme control and focus, despite any distractions, and to know that she'd shattered his concentration was a very heady sensation. "What was the problem?" she asked, much too innocently.

"*You* were the problem," he confirmed softly, irritably.

He stood just inches away, not touching any part of her—not yet, anyway—and it took so much effort on her part not to arch her restless body against his, to rub her aching breasts along his chest and wrap her legs around his hips. She inhaled the scent of his cologne, which wrapped around her like its own caress, increasing the sensual hunger building deep inside of her.

A muscle in his jaw flexed as he continued his rant. "Even after you were gone, I couldn't stop thinking about the bold way you walked into my office and sucked me off, how you so brazenly spread yourself on my desk for me to fuck. All afternoon, I had the smell of you on my fingers, and the taste of you in my mouth. When I should have been working, I was instead thinking about your waxed pussy and how incredible it felt, which made my dick hard at very inconvenient times."

Her mouth twitched with a triumphant smile, which he didn't seemed to appreciate, at all. "I'm sorry."

His gaze narrowed on her face. "I don't think you are."

She bit her bottom lip, knowing that they'd just come to a fork in the road... and this moment could go one of two ways. The conversation could end with flirty banter, or she could open the secret door to all the things she craved with her husband.

For her, it was a no-brainer.

She lifted her chin a few inches, just enough to display a show of defiance. "If I've been so bad, maybe you ought to spank me."

The carnal heat that flared to life in his eyes singed her, and his entire body went absolutely still. "Do *not* tempt me," he said, his voice a low, dark warning.

Oh, he had no idea the *temptation* he was up

ERIKA WILDE

against, or just how persistent she could be in order to get what she wanted, too. "If I was a bad girl today, I should be punished."

He grasped her chin in his fingers, forcing her to see his fierce expression. "You're playing with fire, baby."

Another ominous threat she had no intention of heeding. "Maybe I want to get burned." Such a cliché, but so true. She knew he could make her burn *so* good.

His expression took on a dangerous edge, the kind she suspected had instantly coerced many a man to comply with whatever demand he'd issued. But there was nothing about Dean that she feared, and there was nothing he could do or say to make her back down or retreat.

"Spank me," she whispered huskily. "I *dare* you."

The challenge in her voice, her words, tipped him right into the palm of her hand, just as she'd anticipated. Her husband thrived on thrills, risk and adventure, so how could he say no to one of his own wife's challenges?

The tight clenching of his jaw eased a fraction. "We're not doing this without a safe word."

She automatically shook her head. "We don't need one."

"Yes, we do," he countered resolutely. "If this is the way you want to play, then having a safe word is non-negotiable. It's a deal-breaker, Jillian."

Clearly, this was one area where he absolutely would not compromise. She trusted him, but he didn't trust himself. He needed the reassurance that she could put an end to the act anytime with a carefully chosen word, so there was no confusing playful, breathless begging with the need for him to truly *stop*. For him, a safe word meant she was completely serious.

The fingers on her chin tightened. "Choose one, Jillian."

She heard the make-or-break tone of his voice. If she wanted this—and Lord, did she ever—she had to comply. It was a small concession to make to gain his cooperation. "Mercy."

His mouth twisted with wry amusement. "Appropriate enough, I suppose."

"I thought so."

He finally released her. "Come," he ordered firmly, then turned around and headed for the adjoining family room, obviously expecting her to obey him without question or argument.

After checking once more that she'd turned off the stove, she followed him. He sat down in the center of the wide couch, and motioned for her to stand a few feet away from him. He pulled on the knot of his tie, loosening it from around the collar of his shirt so he could slip the strip of fabric over his head and off, then set the tie on the cushion next to him.

Take off your clothes," he ordered as he released the top three buttons on his shirt, exposing the sexy hollow of his throat and a glimpse of his chiseled chest. "All of them."

She adhered to his request, all too aware of him watching her with hooded eyes as she stripped off her tank top, then her yoga pants. Unhooking her bra—a more practical beige one than the red lace she'd worn earlier today—she tossed it to the floor, then added her silk bikini panties. His darkening gaze took in her full breasts and hardened nipples, then drifted down to her bare mound, endlessly fascinated with her smooth, hairless pussy.

He said nothing as he looked his fill of her naked body, but the erection forming beneath the zipper of his pants spoke volumes and attested to just how affected he was. She stood still, her entire being vibrating with excitement as she awaited his next instruction, allowing him the opportunity to direct the scene about to unfold, however he felt necessary.

With a quiet restraint, he slowly, leisurely unbuckled his belt buckle, then pulled the long, thin strip of leather from the waistband of his slacks. He smacked the strap against his palm, as if testing the strength, the weight, the force of the *sting*. A sinful smiled curved his mouth, and her stomach executed a little flutter at the thought of him using the belt on her tender, untried bottom.

He placed the belt next to the tie, then patted the couch cushion next to his right leg. "I want you to kneel right here."

She moved forward and did as he asked, and as soon as she was in position he put his hand around the nape of her neck and gently guided her down so that she was lying flat across his thighs with her bare butt arranged on his lap. Her upper body and face rested comfortably on the sofa cushion, and she had to admit that she felt incredibly vulnerable in her current face-down, ass-up position. But she wasn't afraid. Just... a little anxious about what to expect this first time.

"Hands behind your back," he ordered.

Unsure what he intended, but very curious to find out, she placed her hands at the small of her back. She felt his silk tie on her skin as he looped the soft fabric around and between her wrists a few times, then tied it off in a loose knot with a small bit of give—just enough so that she could relax her arms and shoulders with ease.

Then he picked up the belt. She tensed, preparing herself for the crack of leather, but he merely stroked the supple strap along the curve of her bottom, teasing her with the possibilities.

"Relax, baby girl," he murmured seductively, speaking the sweet endearment he'd chosen for her back in high school. "I don't think you're quite ready for the belt. Not on your virgin backside, anyways. But I do have another use for it."

He wrapped the strap around her upper thighs and buckled the belt so it was secure and tight and she couldn't move her legs apart at all. With both her arms and legs bound, he truly held all the control.

This wasn't the first time that Dean had tied her hands up during sex play, but restraining her legs was new. They'd just traveled into bondage territory, and she had to admit she liked the element of induced subservience. It fed into her own forbidden fantasies, of being helplessly dominated and forced to endure every pleasurable thing her husband did to her.

But that didn't mean she wasn't a little nervous about that first smack, and her racing heart proved it. As if sensing her unease, he gently glided his left hand down the slope of her spine, petting her like a skittish kitten he wanted to calm. His right hand caressed the back of her thighs, his mellow, feel good caresses lulling her into a state of relaxation.

Only when her entire body was soft and yielding did he issue the first smack to her ass. She gasped in shock at the initial sting of pain radiating across her bottom, which he immediately soothed with another delicate caress, making the anticipation grow once again before he slapped her other cheek. Either that, or he was waiting to see if she'd use her safe word before he allowed himself to go on.

It wasn't going to happen.

Trussed up as she was, she couldn't move, could only endure the sweet, delightful punishment he doled out. He continued to repeat the process, and eventually the biting jolt of pain gave way to mild discomfort, then a pleasant burning sensation that made her pussy throb with excitement and need.

He executed another breath stealing strike of his palm, and this time his fingers followed the slit of her ass all the way down between her secured legs. The moment his fingers touched her aching sex, a rush of moisture spilled out of her, coating his hand and her thighs.

A low, deep, primitive growl escaped him as he wedged two fingers deep inside her. "You're fucking drenched."

Proof of how much this scenario aroused her, just in case he had any doubts. At this point, she was so keyed up she knew it wouldn't take much more for her to orgasm—she was already nearly there—and she squirmed on his lap and lifted her ass a little higher in desperation. "Oh, God, Dean. *Please*," she begged.

Her disobedience earned her another sharp slap. "Be still!"

Oh, Lord, she tried. She bit her bottom lip and forced herself not to move, but everything inside her clamored for release. For every spank he issued, he gave her pussy equal attention, his fingers dipping and exploring and stroking her swollen nether flesh until she was on the edge of climax before he retreated once again.

Her juices flowed, and he spread the slick moisture all the way back up between the crevice of her buttocks, his fingers stopping on that forbidden pucker of flesh, adding a bit of pressure, while his other hand kneaded her sore, tender bottom.

His touch *there* was so foreign and unexpected she stiffened, even as other parts of her mind and body wondered what it would be like to experience back door sex. It was a heady thought, and one she wasn't opposed to.

As if reading her mind, he said, "Someday, I want to fuck you here."

"*Yes*," she whispered, granting him permission for whenever he was ready to explore that particular fantasy.

He groaned, and executed one last smack to her warm, tingling bottom before his fingers delved back into her body and began thrusting in earnest. But this time, he placed his thumb against that unchartered territory, and gradually pushed the tip in an inch, then another. The dual penetration overwhelmed her with a barrage of erotic sensations, heightening that clawing need as the pleasure became so intense she could barely breathe.

She started to pant. She resisted the urge to beg once more, certain he'd stop the decadent torment before she could climax. He was completely and utterly in control of her body, her every response, and she was helpless to do anything but surrender to his provocative ministrations.

She would have thought him immune if it weren't for his own harsh breathing, and the thick prod of his shaft against her hip. He was rock hard, and she took satisfaction in knowing that he was just as turned on and on fire as she was.

While his fingers continued to fuck her and

drive her wild, he administered one last hot, searing slap to her ass, which sent her careening over the precipice of a stunning, mind-bending orgasm. The ecstasy was so intense and all-consuming she screamed her pleasure as she came, harder and longer than she ever thought possible.

Her mind spun, and she was vaguely aware of Dean pushing her hips off the couch so that her knees were on the floor and her upper body remained on the sofa. Standing up, he quickly removed all his clothes then moved behind her, straddling her still bound legs so that his hard, muscular thighs bracketed hers.

He tugged on the tie wrapped around her wrists, releasing her hands but kept the belt intact around her legs. She groaned in relief and stretched her arms out in front of her. Knowing she was in for another wild, rough ride, she closed her eyes and curled her fingers around the back of the couch cushion for something to hang onto, and waited in anticipation for him to fill her up.

She felt the smooth head of his cock run down the crease of her ass, stopping momentarily at the place where he'd been touching just moments ago before sliding lower, where she was wet, swollen, and incredibly sensitive from her orgasm. He slid slowly inside her, but once he was buried to the hilt, he exhaled a raw groan, grabbed her waist, and began thrusting in earnest.

With her thighs strapped together, the fit of him was tight, and she could feel the length of his cock rub along the folds of her sex with each rapid stroke. A multitude of sensations assailed her... the heavy weight of his balls slapping against her thighs, the hard grind of his hips against hers, the friction of his pistoning cock pumping in and out of her.

Now that her hands were free, she was able to arch her back and tilt her hips, allowing him deeper access. She clenched and unclenched her inner muscles around him and tossed her head back as she moaned her pleasure, coaxing him to feel as much as she did.

That discipline of his finally snapped, and with an unrefined curse he moved over her completely, pressing his chest against her back and burying his face against her neck, claiming her in a wholly primitive, ruthless way.

He slid one hand between her legs, his

fingers gliding across her clit, his touch just the right combination of rough and delicate strokes. His other hand twisted in her hair and turned her head, forcing her mouth to meet the demand of his.

His kiss was hot, potent, and tinged with a desperate hunger that delighted her. His desire and lust became her feminine power, and she reveled in it, and what she could do to *him*. Their tongues dueled and his strong, muscular body strained against hers, each slam of his hips driving his shaft deeper than she ever thought possible. His long fingers plied her clit with exquisite finesse, and the tension spiraling tight inside her finally gave way to a climax so violent she nearly blacked out.

He waited until her body was shaking, writhing, and coming apart beneath him before he granted himself the same pleasure. The low, animalistic growl that escaped him vibrated against their still fused lips as his big body shuddered, hands clutching her backside almost painfully as he came with a loud, unrestrained roar, then collapsed against her back, breathing hard.

Her own heart raced, the aftershocks of the

sexual blast still rippling through her body, and his. After a while, he pulled out of her and removed the belt from her thighs, then pulled her up onto the wide, spacious couch with him so that they were laying face-to-face, chest to breasts, her legs entwined with his. She sighed, unable to remember feeling so physically and emotionally sated and content after such a vigorous round of sex.

He lazily skimmed a hand down along her side, tracing the indent of her waist and the curve of her hip, then settled his palm over her bare bottom, which was still warm and sensitive from his spankings.

His grey eyes were dark and uncertain as they stared into hers. "Are you okay?"

She knew what concerned him, that he was worried he'd taken things too far, too fast. "I'm good," she said with a smile. "And before you ask, everything about what we just did was freakin' fantastic."

He raised a dark brow, a more playful side emerging. "You liked being tied up and spanked?"

"I loved it." She placed her hand on his cheek, not afraid to admit just how incredible the power of passion and emotion between them had felt during the act. And now, in the aftermath, she also loved the intimacy, the communication, the connection they were forging. "I liked being spanked by you, and those other things you did, especially knowing it turned you on just as much."

The corner of his mouth lifted in a sinful smile. "Yeah, it did turn me on."

She laughed. "You're so easy," she teased.

The hand on her bottom caressed its way back up her body, until his fingers were threading gently through her hair. "So, what next?" he asked.

"Anything and everything." With him, nothing was off limits, and there wasn't anything she wouldn't at least try. "Surprise me."

"*That* I can definitely do," he murmured, the deep, seductive inflection in his voice making Jill shiver with anticipation.

She couldn't wait to see what happened next.

THE BEAST UNLEASHED

*L*ater that night, while Jillian slept peacefully in their bed, Dean sat in his home office/library sipping a shot of Macallan single malt Scotch while contemplating how his wife's seduction today, and her request to add some spice to their sex life, had opened up a whole Pandora's box of illicit possibilities.

Jillian had no idea the true tendencies he'd held back for so many years for fear that she'd think he was depraved or perverse. But in truth, there were many kinky, erotic things he'd imagined doing with her and to her, and restraining her and spanking her tonight was just the mere tip of the iceberg. There were many more dark, carnal fantasies he wanted to indulge in with her.

Today, she'd tempted the beast within him, roused and awakened that buried need to control and possess, and coaxed him out to play—and his vibrant, sexy wife had enjoyed every single aspect of his dominant behavior.

He smiled to himself as he finished off his drink. Jillian had given them both permission and free rein to explore thier fantasies. Now, there was no turning back from all the erotic pleasures awaiting them.

THE SEDUCTION

A DIARY ENTRY

A **diary entry from Jillian Noble:**
Seducing Dean was much easier than I'd expected. He'd enjoyed our tryst in his office, and I loved the way he'd opened up and took control when he came home later that night. Who knew that getting spanked could be so thrilling and arousing?

Already, I sense a change in my husband, a sexual awareness that keeps my body in a constant state of anticipation whenever he's around. The way he looks at me is hotter, like he's imagining all the things he wants to do to me now that there are no boundaries between us.

I can't wait to see how far he's willing to go in order to pleasure us both.

PATIENCE AND RESTRAINT

I *made reservations for dinner at Bertrand at Mister A's. Be ready to go in two hours. Tonight, you're mine.*

Jillian read the text message from her husband and shivered in anticipation. Short, brief, and to the point. She loved that Dean was being so spontaneous, and she especially liked the possessive slant in his message, which meant there was more to this evening than a romantic meal out. She also appreciated the advance notice, which meant she could take her time getting ready.

She headed up to the master bathroom. After getting undressed, she shaved her legs then ran a hot bath, adding a generous amount of jasmine botanical oil to soften and scent her skin. She piled her long, thick hair atop her head, and once the Jacuzzi tub was filled she immersed herself into the steaming bath, closed her eyes, and let the silky warmth soothe her body. In time, drowsy and relaxed, she dozed off until the most delicious, decadent dream slowly cajoled her awake again.

"Wake up, sleeping beauty," a deep voice whispered huskily, while a large, strong palm curved around her breast beneath the water and skillful fingers plucked at her nipples, making them harden into stiff points.

She moaned softly, struggling between waking up and wanting to see how the tempting fantasy ended. A talented thumb swirled around her sensitive areola before a very masculine hand gently squeezed her breast.

"Open your eyes, baby girl."

Dean's voice beckoned to her, as did the fingers lazily trailing their way down her stomach and around her navel. With effort, she blinked her eyes open and stared into her husband's handsome face. He was sitting on the tiled step beside the tub, his shirt off, half of his tanned arm beneath the surface of water. She frowned, her mind gradually processing the fact that he was home, that she'd fallen asleep, and she wasn't ready for their dinner date yet.

She quickly sat up, nearly sloshing water over the side of the tub. "Oh, my God. Am I late?"

His big hand grasped her thigh, holding her in place when she would have tried to stand up. "No, I'm home early. I wanted to take a shower and shave before we go out, but I came in here and found you taking a nap, looking so sweet and peaceful, and I couldn't resist coaxing you awake."

She settled back down into the silky, scented, now luke-warm water and smiled at Dean. "I'm definitely awake, but I wouldn't mind being coaxed a bit more."

He arched a dark sable brow, a glimpse of humor dancing in the gray depths of his eyes. "You're becoming a shameless hussy."

"You bring out the shameless hussy in me." And since he was her husband, she could be as promiscuous as she dared, which was such an incredibly freeing sensation. "I think you need to finish what you started."

His fingers brushed along the inside of her thigh in a teasing caress. "Do you now?"

"Yes, I do." She opened her legs wider in invitation and moaned when two long fingers slid inside her core and his thumb rubbed oh-so-enticingly against her clitoris.

"Such a demanding, bossy thing." He inclined his head, staring at her thoughtfully for a moment before his expression took on a darker, more commanding edge, the one that made her pulse flutter and her body come alive. "I think you need to learn patience and restraint, and tonight, I'm going to teach you that very important lesson. That good things, like orgasms, come to those who learn to wait."

He curled his free hand around the nape of her neck and tipped her head up, just as his mouth came down on hers. His kiss was slow and deep and breathlessly sexy, the kind that seduced not only the mind, but every erogenous zone in her body. His tongue slid against hers and withdrew, then thrust in again, while his fingers adopted the same lazy in-and-out rhythm in her aching sex.

And like the shameless hussy she was, she moved wantonly against his hand. Her back arched, lifting her breasts out of the water, her nipples tightening as the pleasure built, and built, and built toward a spectacular climax, contradicting his statement that he was going to make her wait.

She gasped against his lips, on the verge of coming... and then his touch, and his mouth, were completely and utterly gone, leaving her bereft and deprived. Those nerve endings he'd roused screamed for release and she couldn't contain the mewling sound of disappointment that escaped her.

Opening her eyes, she stared up at Dean and the smug satisfaction curving his sensual mouth. "You did that on purpose."

"Patience and restraint," he reminded her as he stood up, the outline of his hard cock visible beneath the fabric of his pants.

Brazenly, she skimmed her hands down her stomach and toward her still throbbing pussy as he watched, knowing she could easily finish herself off without his help. Just a few strokes against her clit would be enough to give her body what it desperately craved.

His gaze narrowed and his jaw clenched tight. "Don't you dare give yourself that orgasm I know you want so badly. I'll give it to you when I feel you've earned it."

Jillian shivered at his stern, uncompromising tone. She was so very tempted to disobey, just to suffer whatever delicious consequence he'd dole out, but decided to play this game his way. For now. Clearly, it was going to be a very long, and exciting, night.

"By the way, I laid out what I want you to wear tonight on the bed."

"Oh. Okay." That announcement surprised her, since he'd never selected clothes for her before. She was curious to find out what he envisioned for tonight.

Seemingly convinced that he had her cooperation, he turned away and stripped out of his pants and boxer briefs. Gloriously naked, he turned on the shower, then stepped into the spacious marble and glass enclosure. Since she had a great view of her smokin' hot husband, and he had such a beautiful body, she relaxed for a few minutes longer in the tub and watched as the water sluiced over his muscular chest and down his toned backside.

He washed his hair then soaped himself up, and she was very tempted to join him so she could scrub his back… or stroke the impressive erection he was still sporting, she thought with a pleased smile. After rinsing off, he reached for the shaving cream and absently glanced her way.

Seeing that she was still lounging in the tub, he rapped on the glass and frowned at her. "You need to get moving," he ordered like the drill sergeant he probably was with the military men who worked for him. "I don't want to be late for our reservations."

She rolled her eyes, knowing they had plenty of time. But Dean was a man who liked to be punctual, and Lord forbid they were a few minutes tardy. Then again, if it earned her another spanking…

Sighing to herself, she stood up, got out of the tub, and leisurely dried off with a fluffy towel. After wrapping it around her body, she did her make-up, then rearranged her hair into a loose topknot on her head, leaving a few strands free to frame her face. While Dean finished shaving, she headed into the bedroom to see what attire awaited her.

He'd chosen one of her "little black dresses", one she didn't wear very often because of just how little, and blatantly sexy, it was. The front was actually very modest, with a high neck and long sleeves… but it was the completely backless design that was the true show-stopper and never failed to turn male heads as she walked by. The shimmering stretch fabric molded to her body, and the hem reached mid-thigh. There was no bending over in this dress unless she wanted to flash her girly-bits to everyone.

At least he'd picked out full coverage underwear, instead of a thong or G-string. But the black lace was flimsy and see-through, and considering she couldn't wear a bra with the dress, she ought to shock him and go full-on commando, she thought with a wicked grin. Seriously, though, she was grateful he was *allowing* her to wear panties, and put them on before walking over to her bedroom vanity table and selecting one of the fragrances she only wore on special occasions because it was so expensive.

She picked up the crystal decanter filled with Clive Christian perfume, and dabbed the stopper at the hollow of her throat, behind her ears, between her breasts, along the pulse points in her wrists, and lastly, at the back of her knees. The heady, luxurious scent of jasmine and vanilla swirled around her, potently seductive. She stepped into her dress and was adjusting the long sleeves and hem when Dean strolled out of the bathroom, a towel tucked around his hips, then disappeared into the walk-in closet to change.

She fastened the stiletto heels Dean had chosen for her—black leather straps encrusted in sparkling crystals that criss-crossed over her toes and wrapped around her ankles—and had just finished putting the bare necessities into her little handbag when he came out of the adjoining closet, immaculately dressed in a pair of pressed black slacks and a white linen shirt he'd left open at the collar. She was actually disappointed that he wasn't wearing a tie tonight.

He came up behind her, his gaze meeting hers in the gold filigree mirror framing her vanity table. "You are so beautiful." He strummed his long fingers down her bare back, making her shiver and her nipples pucker tight against the fabric of her dress. "But I think your outfit is missing something."

"A bra?" she asked wryly.

He laughed and pressed a warm, damp kiss to her bare shoulder. "You don't need one. Your breasts are perfect."

No, not perfect, but at least they still had some "perk" left to them and were full enough that they didn't droop. But she knew her unruly nipples were going to be a problem tonight, much to Dean's enjoyment, no doubt.

Moving away, he opened the top drawer in his armoire and withdrew a black velvet box with a distinctive jeweler's name imprinted on top, then came back to her. "*This* is what's missing," he said, and handed her the unexpected present.

Eyes wide with surprise, she took the box, but didn't immediately open it. "What is this?" she asked curiously.

Tonight wasn't a special occasion, and while Dean was a generous man, he rarely bestowed lavish gifts for the hell of it. Not that she was complaining, but it told her that he'd put a lot of thought into tonight... from the restaurant he'd chosen, to what he wanted her to wear, to the spontaneous gift he'd purchased for her.

He shrugged a shoulder, looking both boyish and incredibly irresistible. "It's for you to wear and both of us to enjoy."

Interesting choice of words, she thought.

Dying to know what was inside, she opened the lid and gasped when she saw a gorgeous strand of pink-hued freshwater pearls nestled in black satin. Her heart pounded wildly in her chest as she stared at Dean in awe and delight. "These pearls are absolutely stunning."

"So are you." He lifted the necklace from the box—an incredibly *long* strand of pearls that had to cost a small fortune—then walked behind her again.

He placed the necklace over her head, then wrapped the rope of pearls around her neck twice, so that there were two layers cascading down her bare back. She looked at her reflection. From the front, it appeared as though she was wearing a pearl choker, or a luxurious collar, and while she'd seen many women wear long strands in just this fashion, knowing that Dean had chosen this specific style for her gave Jillian a sense of being *owned*. Especially when he gave the necklace a gentle tug and she felt the slight tightening of the pearls against her throat—as if she was wearing a leash and he was her master.

Tonight, you're mine.

The reminder made her insides go liquid with a forbidden kind of longing.

She lifted her gaze and met his in the mirror, the wicked gleam in his eyes causing another rush of heat to arrow straight between her legs. Oh, he knew *exactly* what he was doing, and had bought this necklace for precisely that impression. He'd put conscious thought and consideration into the gift, which made her wonder what other sexy, erotic predilections traveled through that mind of his.

She had her own secret, naughty fantasies and desires, so it was only fair that Dean had his. But now, with their agreement to explore the more unconventional side of sex, they were able to openly share and enjoy those new, exciting scenarios together. And so far, she liked where this night was headed.

"Don't forget the matching earrings," he murmured, brushing his fingertips along her spine one last time before moving away.

Exhaling a deep breath, she slipped the pearl stud earrings into her lobes, then picked up her clutch purse from the bed. "I'm ready to go."

They drove Dean's silver Aston Martin Vantage coupe, which was a nice treat for Jillian since she was used to driving around in her big Suburban. She loved the close quarters of the sporty two-seater, the sleek, powerful ride it provided, and how the interior smelled so masculine, like warm leather and her husband's own essence. Everything about the car was sexy and arousing, and perfect for a date night out with Dean.

When they arrived at Bertrand at Mister A's, Dean valeted the car, then tucked her hand in his as they walked into the restaurant. It was early evening, and the place was already busy, but since he'd made reservations they were immediately led to their table. As they followed the hostess, Dean splayed his hand against the base of her spine, his touch hot and unmistakably possessive.

Jillian was very aware of the pearls dangling down her back and brushing intermittently against her bare skin—like the stroking caress of warm fingers—and despite her best efforts, the sensual sensation caused her nipples to peak against the fabric of her dress. Couples glanced up at them as they walked by—the women to admire Dean, and men being the visual creatures that they were, their appreciative gazes unerringly dropped to her full, unrestrained breasts, which only made her more aware of her tight nipples.

Admittedly, those bold stares did give her a little thrill and boosted her confidence, but she was more concerned about what Dean thought of those men blatantly ogling her. She glanced at his face, but his unreadable expression gave nothing away.

"Here's the private table you reserved, Mr. Noble," the hostess said, stopping at a cozy booth tucked away in a corner away from the other diners. Their table faced the floor to ceiling glass windows encasing the restaurant and gave them a spectacular view of downtown San Diego. The only lighting was a single candle on the table, which cast flickering shadows and gave the atmosphere a romantic, sensual glow.

"Thank you," he said, and smiled at the younger woman. "This is perfect."

Jillian slid onto the leather seat, and was surprised when Dean sat *across* from her, instead of beside her. She would have preferred a more intimate seating arrangement, where she could touch him and vice-versa, but he clearly had other ideas.

The hostess handed them their dinner menus and a wine list, then announced the night's specials before leaving them alone to peruse their selections. A few minutes later a waiter arrived to take their order—baby lamb chops for her, braised prime beef for Dean, and a bottle of Sauvignon Blanc for them to share. Once their server returned with the wine, poured two glasses, then moved on to another table, Jillian glanced at Dean and contemplated the best way to pose the question she wanted to ask.

His eyes met hers and a slight smile curved his lips. "Something on your mind, wife?"

It was unnerving how well he could read her when his shifting moods were far more difficult to decipher, especially when he made a conscious effort of hiding his emotions, like now. But the uncanny ability to read other people without revealing his own agenda is what had made him such a formidable Navy SEAL, and now, a respected security specialist.

She glanced around, and assured that their table was far enough away from everyone else's and that nobody could eavesdrop on them, she decided to appease her curiosity. "Doesn't it bother you having other men stare at my breasts?"

He stared at her breasts. "No. I told you that you have great tits." He gave a casual shrug, even as his eyes darkened with a simmering heat. "Besides, I like knowing that all those other men are lusting over what's *mine*, while I'm the lucky bastard who gets to take you home and fuck you."

His raw words thrilled her, and she couldn't help but glance around to make sure no one else had been privy to his explicit statement. Grateful that their table was far enough away from the main diners to guarantee complete privacy, she met Dean's gaze and delved a little deeper into this fascinating conversation. "So, you like me being on display?"

He took a slow drink of his wine before

replying. "It definitely adds an element of excitement to know other men want you, but it also brings out my possessive side, too, along with the primal need to bend you over the table and stake my claim on you right here and now so they know you belong to me."

She shivered at the slight threat in his tone, which was softened by the humor glimmering in the depths of his smoky gray eyes. "I'd rather not get banned from our favorite restaurant, so thank you for sparing me that awkward scene."

"For now, anyways," he said in a sexy, lazy drawl. "The evening is still young and I can think of more than one way to make sure you realize exactly *who* you belong to."

She already belonged to Dean... heart, body, and soul, but she knew he wasn't questioning her emotional commitment to him. No, his words were laced with a tempting eroticism that had her pulse racing. Clearly, he was playing a role and creating a fantasy, and his aggressive behavior fit the parameters of tonight's theme of her being "owned" by him.

The cool pearls he'd wrapped around her throat were also a subtle, silent reminder that Dean was the one in control, that she was his to command, and she'd willingly do his bidding. She wasn't submissive or complacent by nature, but there was something about surrendering to his provocative demands that filled her with a heady sense of anticipation and excitement. Pleasing him, arousing him, was her ultimate goal... even if that meant being a slave to every one of his desires.

"By the way, it looks like next week's business trip to Chicago is going to be longer than I'd originally anticipated," Dean said, changing the tone of their conversation. "I'll be gone at least seven to ten days."

She'd been expecting him to be gone a week, max. "Why so long?"

"The political summit was extended," he said, leaning back in his seat as his fingers absently stroked the stem of his wine glass. "I'll be arriving with my guys a few days before the summit starts to set up security detail and surveillance, and it'll take us a day or two afterward to break things down."

Jill never liked when he had to take business trips, especially now that the boys were gone, but she knew and accepted that it was part of his job. Dean and Mac were very "hands on"

when it came to their affluent clients, especially the high ranking officials and Fortune
500 executives who retained their protective
services. All the men that Noble and Associates
hired were elite ex-military professionals who
were capable and intelligent, yet Dean always
liked to be present at the bigger events to
diffuse any potential issues or problems that
might arise.

As much as she'd miss Dean, having him
out of town presented Jill with the perfect
opportunity to take advantage of an idea she'd
conceptualized and wanted to make a reality.
"While you're gone, there's something I'd like
to do," she said tentatively.

His gaze turned curious. "What's that?"

She bit her bottom lip, because she honestly
didn't know how Dean would feel about her
suggestion. "I was thinking about turning our
basement into a playroom."

When they'd built their house, they'd
finished off the basement, making sure that the
spacious area was equipped with a heating and
cooling system, insulation, and lighting just in
case they'd ever decided to make it into a
useable living area, but because the rest of the

house was so large, the room had always remained vacant. Now, it presented the perfect place for the two of them to use as a personal, intimate escape.

Amusement flickered across Dean's expression. "So, you want pin ball machines, a Play-Station, and other games to play with?"

He was being deliberately obtuse, but she saw the unmistakable interest in his gaze. "No, I want a private place for us to *play*."

"Define your version of *play*."

She rolled her eyes, knowing Dean knew damn well what she was referring to. "*Sex games*," she said candidly, so there was no misconstruing what she wanted, just as their waiter arrived with their meals.

Her face flushed with embarrassment as the other man set their plates of food in front of each of them, but if their server overheard her explicit declaration, he had the good manners not to show it. He topped off their glasses with the Sauvignon Blanc, and after making sure there wasn't anything else they needed, he left them alone again.

Before Dean could say anything, Jill forged ahead with her ideas and plans before she lost the nerve. "I love our big sleigh bed, but I want a four poster with slats for restraints, and a place for toys, and extra room for different things you might like and enjoy. And there's this Tantra sex chair that looks interesting, but I certainly don't want it in our bedroom for the boys to see when they visit."

Dean laughed, the sound deep and robust. "Holy shit. Who are you and what happened to my wife?"

"Your wife is ready to expand her sexual horizons, as you well know," she said with a bit of sass, then took a bite of her lamb chop, which was perfectly prepared. "I've been doing some research on the internet, and there's some fun and sexy things I want to do and try."

"I've been doing some research of my own," he said, his tone taking on that dark, delicious edge that never failed to elicit a sharp, electric response from her—and made her wonder what kind of sexual games had piqued *his* interest. "And I wouldn't mind having a private playroom for us to use."

Thrilled to have his approval, she shared some ideas she had in mind while they finished their dinner. The young woman who'd helped

Jill decorate their current house also special-ized in creating fantasy bedrooms, and she'd already had a brief discussion with Stephanie about how they could transform the basement into a classy, decadent den of iniquity. Dean listened to her suggestions as he finished off his meal, but like most men, he didn't have a lot of decorating tips to offer.

"So, what do you think?" she asked enthusi-astically.

Setting his fork and knife on his empty plate, he smiled indulgently at her. "Baby, I trust your taste and your judgment. You have my permission, and carte blanche, to do what-ever you'd like to turn the basement into our playroom."

She beamed at him, and couldn't wait to call Stephanie to get started on her new project. "Thank you."

Their waiter appeared, cleared their plates, and returned to see if they wanted anything for dessert.

"I'll have the lemon layer cake," Jill told the server, which was her favorite.

"Just coffee for me," Dean said.

"You don't want dessert?" she asked once

the waiter was gone, surprised that he hadn't ordered his usual—vanilla bean Crème Brulee.

"Don't worry about me. I'm getting dessert," he murmured seductively.

During dinner, the atmosphere between them had been light and casual, but there was a distinct change in him now. There was no mistaking the seductive vibe radiating from him, or the intense heat in his eyes that was nearly tangible.

"Take off your panties and give them to me," he said.

His blatant, unexpected request made her head spin. "W-w-what?" she stammered, certain she'd misunderstood him.

The corner of his mouth twitched with barely perceptible amusement. "You heard me."

His voice had taken on a dark, authoritative bent, one that told her things were about to get very interesting—*if* she followed through on his command. She glanced furtively around, thankful that no one was paying any attention to them. The dining area was dim, lit only by candlelight, yet the thought of shimmying out of her underwear in a public place, where she could easily get *caught*, left her feeling a little breathless.

"We're in the middle of a restaurant," she pointed out unnecessarily.

"We're at a corner booth against a wall and I have a perfect view of anyone who might come this way, including our waiter. Do it *now*, Jill, and don't make me ask again or there will be consequences to pay later."

He was dead serious. Jillian wasn't afraid of any consequence he might dole out, but she was more intrigued and yes, excited, about what he had in mind for her now, and how far he'd take things. The element of getting discovered mid-act definitely increased the thrill, even though she knew that Dean would never let that happen. But just knowing that the possibility existed made her heart race a bit faster.

Thankful for the linen tablecloth that draped across her lap and afforded her a modicum of privacy, she reached down to the hem of her dress and inched up the fabric to the tops of her thighs, until she was able to hook her thumbs into the elastic band of her panties and pull them down. It took some wriggling and finesse to get the underwear all the way down her legs and around the spiked heels of her shoes, but she managed the feat. Crumpling the evidence in her fist, she glanced around once more to make sure the coast was clear before extending her offering across the table to Dean.

He held the delicate panties in his masculine hand, out in the open, upping the stakes of someone noticing that he'd filched her underwear. His fingers rubbed along the silk, and seemingly finding something that delighted him, he smiled wickedly at her. "They're damp."

Mortification rippled through her. "That's *your* fault for all the touching and sexy talk back at the house, and the orgasm you *didn't* give me. Now *please*, put them away!"

"Poor baby girl," he mocked, humor dancing in his eyes as he ignored her request and instead brought the black lace up to his nose and inhaled. "I love the way you smell. Like vanilla, jasmine, and desire."

Oh, my God. She was going to *die* of pure embarrassment!

He tucked the scrap of fabric into his pants pocket just as their server arrived with her dessert, and his coffee. Dean took a few drinks of the dark, rich roast and let her enjoy three bites of her luscious lemon cake before he continued with his sensual torment.

Beneath the table, he wedged one shoe, then the other, between her stilettos and pushed her legs wide apart, and kept them braced there so there was no possible way she could close her legs, even if she tried. With her dress still bunched high around her upper thighs, she was completely open and exposed. Cool air touched her bare flesh, and she carefully set her fork on her plate, preparing herself for whatever he intended to do next—if it was even possible to guess his next move. Ever since their agreement to spice things up, Dean was full of surprises when it came to what he wanted and desired. Then again, *predictable* was boring, and she was coming to thoroughly enjoy the unexpected where he was concerned.

Anticipation built inside her as she waited for him to do or say something, while he looked so relaxed sitting across from her, so gorgeous and sexy and she *so* didn't trust that challenging glint in his eyes. With good reason...

"Touch yourself," he murmured.

The provocative dare made her stomach do a little flip. The smirk curving the corner of his mouth told her that Dean didn't think she'd have the nerve to follow through with his bold request considering where they were, but she wasn't about to disappoint her husband. And if she drove *him* a little crazy in the process, all the better.

He took another sip of his coffee, watching with interest as her right hand lowered to her lap. She arranged the tablecloth accordingly, then skimmed her fingers along the crease of her thigh, until she reached the apex, where she was already spread wide. Feeling exceptionally naughty, she embraced her inner temptress, met Dean's heated gaze, and slid two fingers along the soft, bare lips of her pussy, damp with the same moisture that had coated her panties.

She purposefully let her lashes drift to half-mast and exhaled a soft, teasing sigh. His fingers tightened around his coffee cup, and his jaw visibly clenched. *Good*. There was no reason why he couldn't be hot and bothered right along with her.

"Are you wet?" he asked in a low, rough growl that made her nipples tighten and peak.

She nodded, stroked a little deeper, and let a barely audible gasp escape her lips. "Yes," she whispered. "Very wet."

His nostrils flared. "Prove it."

She wasn't quite sure what he meant. "How?"

He leaned his upper body across the table, the flickering candlelight accentuating the primal hunger simmering in his smoky gray eyes. "Let me taste you. *That's* my dessert."

She shivered at his assertive tone. It wasn't a polite request... it was a direct order, and she was helpless to deny him what he wanted... what *she* wanted, too. She brought her hand back out from beneath the table and extended it toward him, the tips of her fingers glistening with the evidence he'd asked for. He grasped her wrist in a tight hold, his thumb pressing against the main artery pulsing there as he pulled her hand closer. His gaze did a quick sweep of the area to make certain no one was watching before he parted his lips and sucked two of her fingers into the warm, silky cavern of his mouth.

She shuddered and moaned, much louder than she'd intended. Liquefied heat rushed to her core, and damn him, she couldn't even press her thighs together, or cross her legs to help appease the throbbing ache in between.

"Delicious," Dean said, and with one last swirling lick of his tongue between her fingers, and a few arousing nibbles to the tips, he let her go.

Three seconds later, their waiter was standing tableside while Jill tried to contain her flustered composure. He refilled Dean's coffee, and smiled at the two of them. "Can I get either one of you anything else?"

Dean withdrew a credit card from his wallet and handed it to the server. "Just the check, please."

While Dean handled the bill and signed the receipt, Jill finished her lemon cake, all too aware of the fact that he *still* had her feet anchored securely apart beneath the table.

She pushed her empty plate aside and glanced at Dean, anxious to be alone with him so they could *really* get to some down and dirty action. "Are you ready to go?"

"Not quite yet," he said, his features

taking on those incorrigible bad boy traits that never failed to make her a slave to his every whim. "Since you're nice and wet, I want you to make yourself come. Right here and now."

There was no shock or surprise this time— and what did it say about her that she didn't even hesitate to touch herself again?

Shameless hussy.

Yeah, she was feeling bold and brazen and reckless enough to see just how much Dean could handle. With each scenario or fantasy they explored, it was getting easier and easier to let go of her inhibitions with him, to take things to the extreme knowing that pure bliss would always be her reward. It was like an erotic power play between them—and she didn't mind being the one in control every once in a while.

Holding his gaze, she caressed her fingers along those intimate folds, trusting him to stop her if someone came their way. She circled and rubbed delicately, reawakening the bundle of nerves in her sex. Her clit throbbed in response, and she applied just the right amount of pressure, stroked in precisely the right way, and recognized the tell-tale signs of a gathering orgasm.

She bit her bottom lip to keep from groaning out loud, her head tipping back as a familiar tension coiled tight in her belly, then spread lower in a promising flutter of pleasure...

"Fuck. *Stop!*" Dean hissed in a strained voice.

Certain they were about to be interrupted, she immediately ceased touching herself, which effectively, and abruptly, stopped the impending climax she'd been on the very precipice of enjoying.

She swallowed back a moan of disappointment and instead inhaled a deep breath, trying to calm her rapidly beating heart. Unfortunately, there was nothing she could do to quell the need still pulsing between her legs.

She waited for someone to walk past their table, but it never happened. In fact, a quick glance around told her that there had been absolutely no threat of being discovered.

She narrowed her gaze at Dean. "You did that on purpose," she accused softly. "I was *so* close."

"I know." He smiled wickedly, but there was no missing the strain of his own arousal etching his features. "Patience and restraint, baby girl. I told you earlier that *I'd* be the one to give you tonight's orgasm when you've earned it."

Yes, he had, and it just went to show her that *he'd* been in control of this scenario all along, not her.

"*Now*, I'm ready to go." He slid out from his side of the booth and extended a hand to Jill to help her out of her seat.

Fortunately for Dean, the lighting in the dining area was very dim, and his slacks were dark, which helped to conceal the bulge of his erection. Tucking her hand in his, he led her through the restaurant and outside to the cool night air where they waited for valet to deliver his car.

As he navigated the streets toward home with his gaze on the road and one hand gripping the steering wheel, he reached over with his free hand and skimmed his fingers up the inside of her thigh and beneath the hem of her dress, trailing heat and promise in their wake. Immediate need spiked through her, and she opened her legs to him, knowing at this point it wouldn't take much to make her come and hoped that was his plan after making her suffer back at the restaurant.

She should have known better.

His long fingers slid along her swollen, sensitive folds and slipped a few inches inside her, knowing exactly what to do to bring her to that breathless crest before easing off and leaving her wanting so much more. He teased and retreated, over and over again, as if proving to her that *he* was truly the one in control of her pleasure tonight.

It didn't take long before she was nearly panting, her body so primed she wanted to wail in frustration—but she refused to give him that satisfaction. She clutched the edge of her leather seat, her hips undulating, her body arching in an attempt to grasp that orgasm he kept just out of her reach.

Between driving and fingering her, the man was a master at multi-tasking. With each skillful stroke she grew wetter, more excruciatingly aroused, until the need to come finally got the best of her and she decided to make things happen herself.

Just as two digits dipped inside her core once again, she grasped Dean's wrist and pushed his hand firmly against her pussy, forcing his fingers to penetrate her all the way up to his knuckles. Her body clenched around the invasion of those fingers, and a flood of moisture spilled over his hand.

The position of his arm was a little awkward for Dean, but she definitely got his attention. He swore explicitly and the car swerved as he turned sharply into a dark, deserted parking lot. He had to remove his hand to put the car into park and turn off the ignition, but then he was back, his right hand now gripping the upswept hair at the nape of her neck and his other diving back between her legs.

He thrust two fingers deep inside her and jerked her head back, making her scalp tingle. His face loomed in front of hers, dark and intimidating. "So fucking impatient," he growled roughly.

A hint of amusement softened his tone, even as his eyes blazed with animal heat and lust. God, he was so freakin' hot like this. So strong, alpha, and dominant, and she loved that she'd provoked such tempestuous passion from him.

"Make me come, Dean," she pleaded.

A raw groan rumbled out of him, and he sealed his mouth securely over hers, coercing her lips apart so he could kiss her hard and relentlessly deep. The thrust of his tongue matched the same steady, driving rhythm of his fingers. His thumb found her clit, pressed and rubbed, and the slick friction was exactly what she needed to send her reeling. Her climax was intense and sublime, and she went limp against her seat as he released her.

He moved back to his side of the car, his hands going to the waistband of his pants. She heard the hiss of his leather belt in the quiet, shadowed confines of the car, the rasp of his zipper as he quickly pulled it down, then the rustle of his shirt as he hastily pulled it out of the way.

"Suck me off, Jillian. *Now.*"

His voice was harsh and filled with an urgent demand that excited her. She was more than happy to return the favor, and by the time she released her seatbelt and leaned over the console to go down on him, his thick, jutting shaft was waiting for her.

She curled her fingers tight around the base of his cock. Pre-cum seeped from the tip, and she slowly licked it away and playfully swirled her tongue over the swollen head, teasing him, just as he'd teased her all evening long.

"*Suck me*," he ordered sharply, and for the first time in their marriage, he didn't give her a choice. He wrapped the pearls draping down her back around one of his fists until the strands tightened against her neck like a collar, and splayed a strong hand against the back of her head to push her mouth *down*, forcing her to take him all the way to the back of her throat.

She moaned, greedily sucking him as he guided her lips back up the length of his cock before he thrust back in again. His breathing escalated and his hips jerked as he increased the rhythm of each deep stroke as he fucked her mouth, faster, harder, wilder. With the pearls constricting against her neck and his palm controlling the bobbing of her head, she let him take what he wanted, what he needed, and she willingly gave it to him until he finally

erupted with a loud, unrestrained roar of satisfaction.

She took everything Dean had to give, until
he eventually let go of her head and released
the pearls, then collapsed against his seat like a
man who'd just had his world rocked in a
major way.

She pushed back and grinned up at him.
"That was *so* hot," she said, licking the taste of
him from her bottom lip. "Patience and
restraint is *so* over-rated."

He peered down at her through half-mast
lashes and grunted, caveman like. "We'll see
about that. We still have the whole night ahead
of us and I'm not done with you yet."

Jillian couldn't even imagine that Dean had
the energy for more, but the one thing she was
beginning to realize about her husband, his
stamina had returned with a vengeance. And
she planned to take full advantage of it.

PEARLS ARE A GIRL'S BEST FRIEND

*A*s soon as they arrived at home, Dean took Jill's hand and veered in the opposite direction of their bedroom, instead leading her toward his office/library. An odd choice, she thought, but didn't question his preference and silently followed.

Now that they'd taken the edge off of their desires back in that deserted parking lot, she was feeling much more relaxed. But even though the frantic need that had consumed them both had ebbed, there was an air of determination about Dean that increased her awareness of him, and how the rest of the evening would play out.

There was no telling what he had in mind,

and not knowing what lay ahead for her added a thrilling element of suspense that kept her libido humming and her body teeming with sexual tension. She loved how he was gradually revealing true aspects of himself and was finally giving into those darker passions she always knew simmered beneath the surface. It was getting easier for him to take what he wanted, to be aggressive and demanding and be confident in the knowledge that she enjoyed every single thing he did to her.

In just a short time they'd already explored a few erotic fantasies and some kinky behavior that paved the way to more explicit adventures. Spanking her had been enjoyable for the both of them, and his use of force in certain situations was a huge turn on for her. And now, she had his agreement to create a private playroom for the two of them that she couldn't wait to fill with all sorts of sexy things for them to do and try.

They entered his office, and he let go of her hand, leaving her standing in the middle of the room, which smelled like rich, dark leather and the faint scent of his cologne. He didn't turn on the main overhead light, but instead switched on the desk lamp for softer lighting before returning to her.

He grasped her chin between his thumb and forefinger and tipped her face up to meet his serious expression. "After that stunt you pulled in the car, I really ought to bend you over my knee and let you feel the sting of my leather belt across your ass."

Her pulse tripped with way too much excitement. *Oh, yes, please*, she thought, but held back her brazen comment.

"Do you think, from here on out, that you can do what you're told?"

She nodded. "Yes."

His gaze narrowed, as if he didn't fully believe her promise. Considering her show of defiance in the car on the drive home, she didn't blame him for being skeptical.

"I won't tolerate any further disobedience tonight, and there will be consequences for your insubordination, understand?"

She really was going to try and be good. "Yes."

The corner of his mouth twitched with a flicker of amusement. "Yes… what?"

Her initial confusion gave way to understanding, and she gave him what he seemed to want from her, which also established certain roles between them. "Yes, *sir.*"

He skimmed his thumb along her bottom lip, dipping just inside to dampen his finger. "I like the way that sounds coming from you, so soft and breathless."

Jillian was starting to feel *very* breathless. She knew Dean was used to hearing the respectful moniker from the men who worked for him all the time, but there was no mistaking the sexual connotation of her husband insisting *she* call him "sir". The one word established him as her master and put her into the position of submissive. In this kind of setting, she'd surrender to him any way he wished.

He released his hold on her chin. "Take off my shirt," he ordered.

Divesting him of any of his clothing was a pleasurable task she didn't hesitate to perform. First, she unbuttoned the cuffs of his sleeves, then slowly, leisurely repeated the process all the way down the front of his shirt. Once the fabric parted, she pushed the crisp material over his broad shoulders and down his arms, until the garment fluttered to the hardwood floor at his feet.

Unable to resist the urge to touch the sheer perfection that was his chiseled chest, she lifted her hands and splayed them on his pecs. The taut muscle beneath her palms flexed, but before she could skim her hands along his abdomen and explore further, he caught her wrists and stopped her descent.

"Did I say you could touch?" he asked gruffly.

She shook her head. "No... sir."

"Take off your dress," he said brusquely.

He let go of her hands and took a step back, giving her space to strip, and him enough room to watch her get naked. She pulled the shoulders down and slowly peeled away her dress. His gaze turned to molten heat as the fabric slithered down the rest of her body and pooled around her shoes, leaving her standing in front of him in just those decadent pearls draping down her back and her feet strapped into the crystal encrusted stiletto heels.

"You look like a sex kitten," he murmured and moved close again.

She stood still as he trailed his fingers down

the slope of her breast and rubbed the pad of his thumb across her hardened nipple. An uncontrollable shiver rippled down her spine as those skillful fingers continued their sensual caresses along her stomach, then lower still. Holding her gaze, he delved between her thighs and stroked her nether lips, making it very clear that he could touch her whenever, and however, he wanted.

"You're so fucking beautiful, every inch of you," he said, his soft tone reflecting his appreciation as his fingers pushed a little deeper, just enough to tease her. "And right here, you're so soft and wet." He leaned in, pressing his mouth against her ear as he whispered provocatively, "I can't wait to bury myself deep inside your pussy and feel you come around my cock."

Her breathing hitched and she turned her head, dying to kiss him, but he merely skimmed his lips along her jaw, avoiding her mouth completely—proving that he was definitely in charge tonight.

"Take down your hair," he commanded.

It was extremely difficult to concentrate on the task when the hand between her thighs was doing such wicked things to her—rubbing her clit, stroking her sensitive flesh, and making her body desperate for another orgasm.

With shaking fingers, she managed to pull the clips from her hair and the silky, disheveled curls cascaded down her back and around her shoulders. She shook her head to loosen the strands, which caused her breasts to jiggle and the pearls to sway along her spine, adding to the excruciating awareness coursing through her.

His hand fell away, leaving her frustratingly aroused. "Get on your knees," he said, his voice husky and low.

Kneeling in front of him, she lowered her bottom so it rested on the legs folded beneath her, then placed her hands, palms down, on her thighs. He tunneled his fingers into her hair, gripping it tight in his fist at the nape of her neck, and tipped her head up to meet his hot, hungry gaze.

"Good girl," he praised her, clearly pleased with her acquiescence.

Directly in front of her, his thick erection strained against the front of his slacks, and she so wanted to pleasure him like this—on her knees in a submissive position with him holding all the power and control. He seemed to consider it for a moment, then untangled his fingers from her hair and walked away toward the wet bar, his gorgeous, bare back to her as he poured himself a double shot of his favorite Scotch from a crystal decanter.

She remained where she was, growing inwardly impatient as he settled into a large cushioned chair across the room. Legs sprawled wide, he stared at her, as if contemplating what to do next—though she was certain he already knew. Cool, calm, and collected, he took a drink of his Scotch, set the glass on the table next to the chair, and finally spoke again.

"I want you to crawl over to me on your hands and knees, *slowly*," he instructed.

Oh, my. Here was her chance to unravel Dean's staunch composure a bit, to tempt and tantalize him. Positioning herself on her hands and knees, she started moving toward him at a leisurely pace, her legs stretching out behind her as her palms slid along the polished wooden floor. Emboldened by the tell-tale clench of his jaw as he watched her approach, she put an extra sway in her hips and gave him a sultry, seductive, I-want-to-eat-you-up smile.

The pearls around her neck fell forward, bouncing against her bare breasts and brushing across her sensitive nipples like a lover's caress. She felt incredibly sexy and a little slutty crawling toward Dean in nothing more than pearls and fuck-me stilettos, and reveled in the raw hunger transforming his features. She skimmed her tongue across her bottom lip, delighting in the feminine power that was hers for the moment, even though she knew it wouldn't last long.

Reaching his chair, she came to a stop and resumed her kneeling position, awaiting his next order.

"You're quite a tease." He took another long drink of his Scotch, his gaze hot and searing as it met hers. "Strip off the rest of my clothes."

She did as he asked, starting with his shoes, then his socks. She rose up between his spread legs so she could reach the waistband of his trousers, and quickly unbuckled his belt, then lowered the zipper over the granite column of his erection. She pulled off his pants and boxer briefs simultaneously, and he helped the process by lifting his hips so she could easily drag them down his thighs and long legs.

A soft sigh of appreciation escaped her as she took in the sculpted body he kept in tip-top shape. Wide shoulders tapered down to a narrow waist, and his lean, muscular thighs provided a perfect frame for the jutting length of manhood between. Her fingers itched to touch his cock, but she curbed the impulse. Just barely.

Dean crooked a finger at her. "Come up here and sit on my lap, facing me."

She stood back up and sat astride his thighs, her knees tucking against his hips. He pulled her forward a few more inches, deliberately nestling his rigid shaft against the swollen lips of her sex when she'd much rather have him buried deep inside. Hopefully, soon.

He lifted the long strand of pearls up and over her head, removing them. "Put your hands behind your back," he murmured.

She followed his command and he reached behind her, looping and knotting the long strand around her wrists until her hands were secured tight together. The position of her arms pulled her shoulders back and thrust her breasts forward, closer to Dean's face.

"Lift up on your knees."

Again, she obeyed, rising up so that she was poised over his cock. She fully expected him to push inside her, but instead he pulled the last of the pearls between the crevice of her ass and down along the soft folds of her pussy, so that the cool, smooth beads rolled against her ultra-sensitive flesh like an intimate kiss. With the rest of the length, he wrapped and twisted the strand around the base of his erect penis, looping it twice so it hugged his erection like a make-shift cock-ring. The man was so full of surprises and more innovative than MacGyver, and she was impressed with his clever use of the pearls.

"Now, I want you to sit on my cock," he said, grasping her hips to guide her downward. "Slow and easy."

She sank onto that thick column of flesh, straddling him completely, taking all eight inches until he was seated to the hilt and the pearls created a cache of erotic sensation between them. She loved how the strand of pearls connected them, how those lustrous beads gave them both varying degrees of plea-sure. For her, the pearls massaged her clit with the slightest movement, and she rocked her hips forward, gasping as a new, provocative kind of friction added to the delicious torture.

Dean growled in response and grasped her waist to stop her lap dance, his gray eyes dark-ening like an oncoming storm. "Don't move until I say you can," he bit out roughly. "Do you understand?"

So, he was going to prolong the sensual torment. "Yes, sir."

Satisfied that he had her cooperation, he let go of her and dipped two of his fingers into his glass of Scotch on the side table. Once they were dripping wet, he spread the liquor onto one nipple, then the other, before leaning forward and sweeping his tongue across the beaded crest in a long, slow lick that made her entire body shudder and her head fall back on her shoulders. Filling both of his hands with her breasts, he squeezed the soft flesh as he licked each nipple, swirling his tongue around her areole, then sucking her deep inside his hot, wet mouth.

She moaned, and despite his order to stay

still, her back arched, pushing her breasts more fully against his lips. The position caused the pearls to tug along her bottom, to rub against her aching sex, and tighten around his cock in a delightful way that made him groan, too.

Her disobedience earned her a sharp nip of his teeth on her nipple, and shockingly, that sting of pain made her pulse deep inside, making her even more restless, incredibly aroused, and beyond desperate to *move*.

He released her breasts and once again soaked his fingers in the Scotch. Eyes latched onto hers, he blazed a wet trail down her stomach, over her mound, then delved between her spread legs. He stroked her clit, using the pearls to increase her pleasure, while making her slick with moisture and need.

"Oh, God, Dean..."

Just when she would have tipped over the edge, he stopped caressing her. Removing his hand, he lifted his damp fingers to her lips.

"Taste yourself," he ordered huskily, and pushed two long fingers into her mouth, giving her no choice but to comply. She sucked lightly, savoring the combined flavors of the Scotch's smoky oak undertones and her own unique essence. His pupils dilated as she continued to swirl her tongue and felate his fingers.

With a low, deep rumbling sound that reverberated in his chest, he pulled his hand away and slid his palm around the nape of her neck, bringing her mouth to his for a kiss. She expected the merging of their lips to be as wild and feverish as she felt inside, but Dean did the exact opposite. He kissed her slow and deep, the kind of joining that made her melt against him, inside and out.

Even though their bodies were intimately fused and she could feel him throbbing deep inside of her, neither one of them moved. It was an incredibly erotic sensation being filled so full, yet denying the basic need to gyrate against him, to feel his length sliding in and out of her and driving her to the precipice of the orgasm simmering just beneath the surface.

It had been a very long time since they'd indulge in prolonged foreplay, and he'd managed to not only heighten her sexual antic-ipation, but tonight had forged an intimate connection between them—not just physically, but emotionally, too. Her soul felt possessed by him, her heart and body his for the taking.

In time, his hands traveled down to her hips and he began a slow rocking motion of their bodies that mimicked the escalating hunger of their kisses. She let him set the pace, let him make love to her at his leisure, knowing it was just a matter of time before the growing ecstasy and need between them became more than his body could deny.

The thrust of his tongue became more aggressive, and the grip on her waist tightened as his hips jerked upward, plowing into her harder, faster—driving so deep she gasped and groaned against his ravenous mouth. The hands secured behind her back moved restlessly, causing the pearls to tug and pull, elevating the friction around his cock and against her clit and pushing them both to the point of no return.

They climaxed simultaneously—a glorious, decadent, earth-shattering explosion unlike anything in recent memory. The force of their release ripped a raw, primitive groan from Dean, and Jillian came with a soft keening cry of pure joy. When the intensity ebbed she collapsed against his chest and buried her face against his throat, both of them gasping for breath.

"Holy shit," Dean rasped against her cheek. "That was—"

"Phenomenal?" she supplied for him.

"I was going to say fucking amazing, but phenomenal works, too," he said, his tone filled with humor. He reached behind her and with a few well-placed tugs on the strand of pearls, he managed to release her hands.

She groaned in gratitude and gingerly eased her arms back in front of her, and placed her palms on his chest.

"Are your shoulders and arms okay?" he asked, clearly concerned that he might have hurt her.

"They're fine," she assured him. Truthfully, they were a little stiff from being trussed up for so long, but it wasn't anything she couldn't handle.

She lifted her head from the crook of his neck and met his very sated expression. "You like restraining me, don't you?" Between him tying her hands when he'd spanked her and again this evening with the pearls, bondage was becoming a common theme with him—one she enjoyed, as well.

"Yeah, I do," he admitted huskily.

"Why?" She was curious to hear his explanation, to know the reasons why having her at his complete mercy excited him so much.

He absently skimmed his fingers up and down her spine in a feathery caress. "Because it forces you to relinquish complete control, to let me do whatever I please so you don't have a choice and no desire remains hidden," he replied honestly.

Ahhh, but she knew she *always* had a choice —along with a safe word he'd immediately heed. That was the safety net that allowed her to let go of her own inhibitions, to make herself vulnerable to him in ways that deepened the emotional bond between them.

"I like being restrained," she told him, just in case he had any doubts.

"I know," he said, much too confidently.

She laughed at his arrogance and shifted on his lap, feeling the smooth strand of beads roll between their still connected bodies. "Thank you for the pearls," she said, a smile tipping up the corner of her mouth as she stared at his handsome features. "Whoever coined the phrase that diamonds are a girl's best friend clearly had no idea just how pleasurable pearls could be. I didn't realize they had so many uses."

"Oh, you have no idea," he murmured incorrigibly as he gently pushed her disheveled hair away from her face, then trailed his fingers along her jawline. "Maybe next time I'll push them deep inside of you and pull them out slowly, one by one, while going down on you and making you come."

She shivered at the intoxicating thought. "Maybe I'll let you."

He chuckled softly. "What makes you think I'd give you a choice?"

She rolled her eyes but didn't argue, instead opting to let him believe that he was the alpha male in their marriage. "I'm going to miss you next week while you're gone for work."

"I'll miss you, too," he admitted in a gruff tone before lightening the moment with a grin. "But you know what they say about absence making the heart grow fonder."

"And the sexual anticipation stronger," she added, waggling her brows lasciviously.

His gaze heated with agreement. "That means by the time I get home, you're going to be in *big* trouble."

"Oh, I do hope so," she breathed against his lips before sealing that promise with a kiss.

WATCH ME

*D*ean walked into his hotel suite after a long day of security and surveillance at the political summit Noble & Associates had been contracted to attend. So far, the event had been straightforward and routine for him and his men, which was just how he liked things to go—without any unplanned disturbances or incidents for the high ranking officials they were hired to provide protection for.

He shrugged out of his suit jacket, then tugged at the restricting tie around his neck, loosening the strip of fabric so he could pull it off—reminded, as always, just how useful a tie could be when it came to restraining his wife and just how much she enjoyed being bound for his pleasure. A necktie was a nice, safe start to bondage, as were pearls, and now that he knew just how much being constrained turned her on, he couldn't stop imagining all the other kinky things he wanted to explore with her, and do to her.

The possibilities were endless.

In the past few weeks since Jillian had walked into his office, stripped for him, and blown his mind with her seduction tactics, his wife had become an insatiable temptress straight out of his deepest, most private fantasies—uninhibited, risqué, and open to all sorts of provocative, exciting adventures. After nineteen years of marriage, he was having the hottest, most passionate and erotic sex of his life with a woman he couldn't seem to get enough of.

Damn, he was a lucky bastard, he thought with a smile.

He knew the emotional component between them was a key element to this new sexual odyssey they were embarking upon, as was Jillian's trust that allowed her to surrender herself completely to his carnal demands. As a woman, she was strong and capable in everyday life, but as his wife, he liked that she was willing, and eagerly so, to let him take control in the bedroom.

Because of her coaxing, he could feel a piece of himself that he'd always held back gradually rising to the surface, encompassing deeper, darker needs he'd denied for much too long. It was as though she instinctively knew about those wicked desires of his, and wanted to explore all those nuances with him. Jillian's acceptance and understanding, along with her own secret fantasies she was gradually revealing, made it so much easier to embrace his more dominant nature and give them what they *both* wanted.

With each sexual encounter they role-played, they went a bit farther, testing all those boundaries that they'd never dared to push past before. Their sex life had always been pleasurable, but now it was intense and incendiary and addicting—and his wife was his drug of choice. The more he had Jillian, the more he wanted her, and being physically away from her for ten days was killing him.

He'd talked to Jillian on the phone every

night since leaving for the summit, filling her in on the day's events and listening to her ideas about the new playroom her girlfriend was helping her furnish and decorate while he was gone. Tonight, he wanted more than casual conversation, and apparently, so did Jillian, because she'd sent him a text earlier that afternoon with a suggestion he hadn't been able to resist: *Skype with me tonight?* He'd replied with an unequivocal *yes*, then had spent way too much time imagining how to best take advantage of the situation.

He had a few sexy ideas in mind, and he powered up his laptop while he stripped off the rest of his clothes and pulled on a comfortable pair of gym shorts. It was past ten at night in Chicago, and the two hour difference made it eight o'clock in California, which was right around the time they normally talked by phone.

As soon as his computer was finished booting up, he sat down in an armchair, propped his feet up on the footstool, and set the laptop on his thighs. He clicked on the Skype icon on his desktop, and as soon as the program was open and he could see that Jillian was already online, he sent a message to her to connect the call. A few seconds later, her pretty face appeared on his screen.

She was lying casually on her stomach on their bed, her laptop in front of her, a happy-to-see-you smile on her lips as his own image appeared on her monitor. "Hey, baby," she greeted him. "How was your day?"

"Busy, but good," he replied. "How about yours?"

"Same here. Stephanie and I found the most amazing four poster bed for our playroom," she said, her eyes alight with excitement. "It's hand-crafted by a local artisan who also makes pieces of erotic furniture on the side, so the bed frame has quite a few *extras* build into the design. I can't wait for you to see it."

He smiled, enjoying her enthusiasm. "Just make sure it has slats or posts for me to tie you to the bed," he said wickedly.

She laughed, the sound light and teasing. "Oh, it most certainly does. And they're strong and thick enough to keep you restrained, too," she added with a bit of sass.

He arched a brow, realizing that she might have her own in-control-fantasy in mind. "You have to pin me down first before you can tie me up, baby girl."

"I'm definitely up for the challenge; though I have a feeling you wouldn't resist *that* much."

No, it wouldn't be a hardship to be the recipient of whatever pleasures his wife might inflict on him while he was restrained, though he didn't want her to think he was *easy*. "You'll have to wait and find out."

"I bought something I want to show you," she said, and moved off the bed to retrieve the item.

She returned a few seconds later and sat down, cross-legged, on the mattress in front of the laptop, her gorgeous hair falling haphazardly around her shoulders. He noticed she was wearing one of his buttoned up linen shirts that he wore for work, which she did occasionally when she wanted to get his motor running. She knew how much it turned him on to see her in his shirts—it was like a male, territorial mark of possession on his woman— and he wasn't immune to its effects now. She'd deliberately left the top four or five buttons undone to give him a glimpse of something red and lacy beneath, and with her legs crossed, the hem barely reached mid-thigh, providing him with another risqué flash of matching red panties.

Holy hell. His dick responded accordingly, growing hard from the mere sneak peek.

"Isn't it just stunning?" Jillian asked, yanking his gaze from between her legs to the item she was holding for him to see.

He hadn't known what to expect, but the fact that she was showing him a vase totally threw him off. Sure, it was pretty enough— obviously a hand blown glass piece with deep purple and green swirls in the pattern and a wide scalloped rim, but it was a *vase*. He honestly didn't give a shit, but Jillian looked so delighted with her purchase that he didn't want to deflate her adorable enthusiasm.

"Nice vase," he said, trying to inject some kind of interest into his voice. "Is that a hint for me to bring you home flowers more often?"

"No," she said, laughing. "Technically, this *is* a vase, but I didn't buy it for flowers. It's to keep in our new playroom and for us to fill with all our secret, private fantasies. We can each write them down, put them in this deco-rative vase, and blindly pick one when we need some inspiration and be surprised by whatever we've chosen. What do you think of that?"

"I love the idea," he said, truly intrigued by the concept. "But just for the record, you're all the inspiration I need."

She grinned flirtatiously. "Ahhh, that kind of flattery will get you everywhere, Mr. Noble."

He chuckled. "I'll keep that in mind, Mrs. Noble."

She reached behind her and set the vase on the nightstand, then glanced back at the webcam, her features taking on a soft, sultry expression. "So, tell me, Mr. Noble. What fantasy do I inspire for you?"

Where did he begin? He'd harbored quite a few erotic ideas when it came to his wife, most of them illicit and shocking, but decided to save those for their new "fantasy vase", and opted for something more relatable, but equally hot.

"Do you remember when we went to dinner and you asked if it bothered me that other men were staring at your braless breasts?"

She nodded. "Yes, and you said that you liked knowing that all those other men were lusting over what was *yours*, while you were the lucky bastard who gets to take me home and do me."

"I believe I said *fuck* you," he corrected, his tone laced with amusement. "But yeah, that's all part of a fantasy I've had about you. I've thought about taking you to a night club wearing something really sexy and watching you dance and flirt with other guys and turning them on, all the while knowing I'd ultimately be the one to bury myself deep inside your sweet cunt."

Her lips parted in surprise—at his explicit words or the suggestion, he wasn't sure.

"You wouldn't get jealous watching me dancing or flirting with another man?"

The intrigue in her voice assured Dean that she wasn't opposed to the idea, and that notion made him hotter than hades. "Hell yeah, I'd get jealous," he said gruffly. "And possessive, and I'd have to stake my claim in a way that would make it very clear exactly who you belong to."

Her chest rose and fell with a deep breath, drawing his gaze to the opening in the shirt she wore and the red lace teasing him like a red cape to a bull. "I like that fantasy," she admitted, her voice soft and aroused. "I'd do that for you."

He was beginning to appreciate that there was probably very little his new, adventurous wife wouldn't try with him, and that was a very heady, powerful realization. "Your turn to share a deep, dark fantasy," he said shifting the tables on her—because he was dying to know what thoughts and images got her off.

She bit her bottom lip, and he watched a delightful pink flush tint her complexion. Her hesitation made him all the more curious. "Come on, sweetheart," he cajoled in a lazy drawl. "Spill your secrets."

"I've always had a stranger/captive fantasy," she revealed, her voice husky as she stared into the webcam. "Like an intruder who breaks into the house, ties me up, then coerces me to surrender to whatever he wants or desires."

Jesus. Dean hadn't seen that one coming. His blood heated in his veins as his mind conjured up those erotic images, of being the stranger who stalked her, and eventually captured her, then bent her to his will for his pleasure. The scene was all about danger, a bit of roughness, and *consensual* force, but her fantasy played right into those dominant urges of his and appealed to him just as much.

She sighed and her legs shifted restlessly beneath her, causing the hem of his shirt to slip a bit higher on her thighs. "All this talk about fantasies is getting me hot and bothered," she said, her tone taking on a seductive quality. "I wish I was there with you right now."

"What would you do if you were?" he asked, giving her the opportunity to take the direction of this conversation any way she wished.

"Anything you asked," she whispered.

She tempted him beyond reason, making him wish he could reach through the laptop monitor and pull her through the portal separating them so she was really there with him. Since that was impossible, he opted for the next best thing. Skype sex.

"You can do something for me now," he said.

She tipped her head, blinking oh-so-innocently. "What's that?"

"Pleasure yourself while I watch."

"How about we make it mutual?" she suggested, an irresistible smile curving her lips. "I want to watch you, too."

He groaned, not sure he'd last long once he started stroking himself. "Okay," he agreed, then added a small qualifier. "But let me watch you just for a little bit first, before I join in. And take off the shirt so I can finally see what you're wearing beneath."

She came up onto her knees, and careful to stay in full view of the webcam, she started slowly unbuttoning the shirt, until the two sides finally separated. She pushed them apart, then shrugged her shoulders, letting the material slide down her arms to reveal a red bra and matching panties.

A whole lot of blood rushed south, tightening his groin with a nearly painful throb. Both undergarments were made of sheer, wispy lace, more to tease than to cover any essentials. Both pieces were unlined, enabling him to see her skin beneath, along with the dusky rose hue of her aureoles, the taut pink nipples, and her bare mound. Her thighs were pressed together, way too prim and proper for this scenario.

"Spread your knees for me, baby," he said, his voice already reflecting a deep rasp of hunger. "Pretend I'm not even here and touch yourself in all the ways that feel good."

She widened her sitting position, giving him a clear view all the way up the vee of her legs, to that scrap of scarlet lace that was already damp with her own desire. Staring straight into the webcam, as if she were making direct contact with his own gaze, she slipped the straps of her bra off her shoulders and let them fall down her arms, until they caught at her elbows.

With one hand, she pushed one of the lace cups aside, exposing a full, gorgeous breast. She caressed the supple flesh in her palm, circled her finger around the crest, then pinched her nipple between her fingers. Her soft gasp was nearly his undoing, until she trailed her other hand down her stomach then into the front panel of her panties and moaned, long and low, as she touched herself intimately, losing herself in her own sensual gratification.

His dick felt like granite and strained against the fabric of his gym shorts, demanding the grip of his fist, which he could no longer deny. Setting his laptop on the footstool in front of his chair, he made sure he still had a clear view of Jillian on the monitor. He quickly removed his shorts, then leaned back and situated himself so she could see all of him, too, on her end. The laptop's camera provided her with a sweeping look of his naked body, from his thighs to the top of his head, and everything in between.

He took his cock in hand, his thumb skimming over the pre-cum seeping from the swollen head to spread the lubricant down the hot, hard length of his erection. Through lashes that had fallen half-mast, Jillian kept her gaze on her own monitor, her breathing turning to a pant as she watched the up and down motion of his fist as he jacked off to her very provocative show.

Beneath the lace, she continued to stroke herself while her other hand squeezed her breasts and her fingers plucked her nipples, tugging on the pebbled flesh in a way that made him think that she just might enjoy the pinch of nipple clamps. The thought made the muscles in his stomach clench and caused his cock to jerk in his tight grip.

"*Dean*," she whispered raggedly as her back arched and her head fell back, her intimate touch growing more frenetic as she concentrated fully on the sensations moving through her body.

He felt like a voyeur watching his own personal porn flick starring his sexy wife, and the incredible vision of Jillian lost in her own pleasure was so fucking hot and erotic he knew he wasn't going to last much longer without erupting like a freakin' volcano. His balls drew up tight and his thighs tensed, bracing for impact and the searing release simmering just beneath the surface.

"*Come*, Jillian," he ordered in a low growl.

She whimpered her need, her hips gyrating faster against her fingers, then her entire body shuddered as her orgasm rocked through her. In the throes of ecstasy, she cried out, unashamed and uninhibited, and it was an incredible sight to behold.

Oh, fuck, yeah. He pumped his cock with firm, rapid strokes, and a deep groan ripped from his chest as he gave himself over to his own robust climax. The hot splash of his release jetted onto his stomach as he came so hard he heard ringing in his ears and his heart felt as though it was going to burst from his chest.

He sagged back against the chair, feeling completely and totally wasted. With effort, he reached for the box of tissues on the table next to his chair and cleaned himself up, then put his gym shorts back on while Jillian made herself more comfortable on their bed.

When he was done and his laptop was settled back on his thighs, he glanced at the monitor to see that she'd propped herself against the headboard with a few pillows plumped behind her, and the comforter was now pulled up to her waist. She was still wearing the red lace bra, but the cups were now covering her breasts, offering her a modicum of modesty.

She adjusted the angle of her webcam so that it was more focused on her face, which was flushed pink and glowing from her recent orgasm. "That was pretty fantastic," she said on a soft sigh of satisfaction. "We definitely need to do that more often when you're on one of your trips."

He couldn't agree more. "Yeah, and now I know *exactly* what you do when I'm not there."

A sinful gleam shimmered in her eyes. "You don't know *everything*. Do you remember that vibrator we bought a few years ago to play around with?" she asked suggestively.

He held up a hand to stop her and groaned. "Do *not* torture me with the details or I'll never be able to sleep tonight."

She laughed softly. "Don't worry, it's a poor substitute for you."

He grinned. "That's good to know."

Dean knew most men would feel threatened knowing that their wives used a vibrating toy without them, but he was confident enough in his masculinity, and certainly open minded enough, to realize that a vibrator came in handy for a woman when a guy wasn't around to provide the real deal.

"I can't wait for you to get home," she said wistfully. "I've missed you."

"I've missed you, too." He wanted to sleep in his own bed at night, curled up against Jillian's soft, warm body. "I'll be home soon, baby girl," he said affectionately.

A few more days, and then he'd be able to fulfill the chase and capture fantasy she'd shared.

THE TAKING

A DIARY ENTRY

a diary entry from Jillian Noble:
After being gone for nearly ten days on a business trip, Dean is coming home today and I can't wait to see him. I've missed him and our time together, though that night we turned up the heat on Skype was definitely hot, thrilling, and fun. I love being uninhibited with Dean, and I certainly enjoyed watching the effect I had on him, too.

The new playroom is almost done. Just a few more final touches and we'll be able to fulfill all sorts of sinful fantasies and indulge in an assortment of erotic kinks. I'm getting excited just thinking about all the possibilities.

HIDE AND SEEK

I'm on my way home. I want the house dark. Hide from me, but when I find you, no matter how hard you fight or resist me, I'm going to fuck you. Hard. Safe word: Mercy.

Jillian sucked in a quick breath as she finished reading Dean's text, her entire body vibrating to life at the realization that her husband was about to take the stranger/captive fantasy she'd divulged to him just a few nights ago and make it a reality. Knowing she only had a matter of minutes to turn off all the lights and make herself scarce before he arrived, she hurried through the house and plunged it into complete pitch black.

Just as she switched off the final lamp in her

small reading nook she heard the garage door leading into the house open then close again with a soft click. Her heart leapt into her throat and she froze, waiting for her pupils to adjust to the sudden darkness so she could move without bumping into anything and alerting *the intruder* of her location.

"Honey, I'm home," he murmured in a low, taunting tone of voice that made her shiver.

Remaining still and quiet, she listened to the light tapping of his steps against the hardwood floor, thankfully heading in the opposite direction. Then the sound ceased and she was pretty sure he'd taken off his shoes to give him a better advantage. It also made it more difficult for her to determine where he was, too, which increased the anticipation building inside her.

Feeling much too vulnerable in the tiny room with nowhere to hide, she moved to the doorway and glanced down the long hallway leading to the main rooms. From what she could see the corridor was clear, and on bare feet she silently made her way to the living room. The entire house was dark, shadowy, and eerily quiet, giving it an ominous feel that enhanced the fantasy of a stalker intent on playing a provocative game of cat and mouse with her.

She reached the living room and was debating whether to duck behind the couch or head to the master bedroom on the opposite end of the house when a large silhouette stepped into her view. Despite knowing this was all a pretense, her mind registered *stranger*, and with a shriek of panic she whirled around to bolt away.

He lunged after her, and she was no match for his speed and agility. Jillian's breath squeezed out of her lungs as he banded his strong arms around her from behind, pinning her arms to her sides and lifting her feet off the floor so she was suspended with no way to escape. A crazy combination of fear and excitement spiked through her and she thrashed her legs, landing a swift kick to his shin. He grunted upon impact, and with a deep-throated growl he set her back on the ground, spun her around, and pushed her up against the nearest wall.

She continued her struggle to escape, but he was so damn strong and so well trained—in martial arts and as an ex-Navy SEAL—that her efforts were futile at best. He grasped both of her hands and pulled them behind her back so they were trapped against the wall and the small of her spine, then he wedged a hard, muscular thigh between hers so she couldn't move her legs. His hips and chest pinned the rest of her body, rendering her completely immobile as he brought his shadowed face so close to hers that she could see the clench of his jaw and the heat and lust glittering in his eyes.

This was *her* fantasy, but he was just as turned on by the scenario. Clearly, he was enjoying the control and power inherent in the situation, along with her coerced obedience, but she wasn't about to surrender so easily, even as she remembered his explicit text: *No matter how hard you fight or resist me, I'm going to fuck you. Hard.*

The inevitable made her pulse race, and she jerked against him, trying to twist her way out of his hold, but his superior physical strength kept her firmly in place. She caught a glimpse of a cocky smile as he secured both of her wrists in one of his big hands, then lifted his other hand up to her face. He framed her chin and jaw with his fingers, forcing her head back against the wall as his mouth came down hard on hers.

The kiss was unapologetically rough, brutally possessive, and it rocked her to the core and set her on fire. His firm lips pushed hers apart and his tongue thrust inside, delving deep and claiming her mouth in a way that declared, *you are mine*. She could taste his hunger, could feel his rising need, even as he maintained complete control of her and the forced seduction aspect of her fantasy.

The hand imprisoning her jaw slowly slid down the column of her neck in an unyielding caress before his fingers encircled her throat, exerting just enough pressure to restrict her breathing for a few seconds and make her imagination run wild. Before full blown panic could take hold, he loosened his grip and continued skimming his palm along her heaving chest until he reached the first button on her blouse.

With an animalistic sounding growl, he ended the kiss and lifted his head, his ominous expression sending a tremor through her and placing him right back into the role of stranger. Gripping one side of her blouse, he yanked hard—once, twice, three times—savagely ripping open her shirt. She gasped in shock, her eyes widening as tearing fabric rent the air and she heard the distinct *ping* of her buttons skittering across the hardwood floor.

With her hands still locked behind her back and his lower body restraining hers, she was helpless against his assault, and the smug look on his face told her he knew he had the upper hand, too. He roughly pulled down one side of her bra, exposing a breast, and didn't hesitate to lower his head and take the plump flesh between his parted lips. His tongue flicked across the stiffening crest, his mouth sucked *hard*, and then his teeth bit down on her burgeoning nipple.

White heat shot through her like an electrical charge, both exhilarating and frightening in its intensity, and she cried out, riding that sharp edge between true pain and exquisite pleasure. Instinctively, she bucked her hips against Dean's in an attempt to somehow escape the sweet, agonizing torment he was inflicting, but his big, muscular body didn't so much as budge. There was no breaking away until he allowed her to.

While his mouth, tongue, and teeth continued to tease her nipple, he reached between their bodies and unsnapped her shorts, then unzipped them a few inches until he had just enough room to push his way inside her panties and shove his hand down between her spread legs. He gave her only seconds to process his touch before he thrust two long fingers deep inside her, stealing her next breath right along with her sense of time or place as he fucked her with those same fingers, mercilessly deep and shockingly rough.

Her inner muscles contracted shamelessly around the thick, ruthless invasion. His tongue flicked across her stiff nipple as he pressed his thumb against her throbbing clit, rubbing and circling, making her forget that she was supposed to put up at least a token fight. Her head fell back against the wall, and she whimpered as his mouth released her breast.

His warm, damp lips skimmed a path up to her neck, the light stubble on his jaw abrading her skin in the most delicious way. "You're so fucking wet," he growled against her ear. "You like this, don't you? Being trapped, your hands restrained, forced to endure a stranger's touch."

Oh, yes, she did. It was a heady fantasy come to life. "No," she said with a shake of her head while trying to inject a believable amount of distress into her voice.

"Liar. Your mouth says one thing, but your soft, wet cunt says something altogether different." He pumped his fingers into her and dragged them back out slowly, and even *she* could feel her body's reluctance to let him go. "You want this."

Yes, yes, yes. "No," she rasped.

He lifted his head and stared at her face, his gaze dark and piercing. His features were shadowed, making it much too easy for her to believe that he truly was an intruder intent on making her his captive. "I've been watching you, following you for weeks, thinking how good it's going to feel when I bury my cock deep inside your tight pussy," he murmured huskily, effectively creating a scenario of her being stalked by him. "Now that I have you, I'm going to spread you wide and take you hard, and you're going to accept everything I have to give. It'll go much easier for you if I have your cooperation, but either way, I *will* be fucking you."

His erotic promise intensified the fantasy, made her pulse trip in anticipation. "I'll be good," she pleaded softly. "Please . . . just release me."

He gradually and oh-so-excruciatingly slowly removed his fingers from her body, and she had to bite back a whimper at the loss of his touch. He eased away from her, a wicked smile curving the corners of his mouth. "Get on your knees and suck my cock," he demanded brusquely.

Clearly, he expected her to drop to her knees and obey, but what was the fun in being docile? Taking advantage of the space between them, she shoved hard at his chest, catching him off guard so that he stepped back to catch his balance, giving her the few precious seconds she needed to flee. She bolted side-ways and came up short as he grabbed a handful of her blouse, jerking her to a stop. Trepidation took hold, and thinking fast she straightened her arms so that her top slid completely off, leaving him holding the torn fabric as she dashed toward the opposite end of the house in just her bra and unsnapped shorts.

She didn't look behind her as she darted into the last available room—his office—and headed toward his large, sturdy, mahogany desk outlined in the dim room. Ducking into the cubby beneath the desk, she pulled his leather chair back into place to conceal her hiding spot. Wrapping her arms around her up-drawn knees, she inhaled slowly, trying to calm her erratic breathing while remaining utterly still and quiet.

Long minutes passed and the dangerous thrill of being caught escalated as she strained to hear movement in the room, but the man was stealthy, and it wasn't until he rounded the desk and she saw the shadow of his legs and bare feet that she knew it was only a matter of seconds before he discovered where she'd hidden.

"Come out, come out, wherever you are," he cajoled in a soft menacing tone that sent all sorts of wild shivers up her spine. The chair rolled away from the desk and he crouched down, his gray eyes glittering with satisfaction when he found her huddled beneath. *"Gotcha,"* he murmured, a wolfish, I'm-going-to-eat-you-up smile curving his lips.

Feeling trapped, her heart seized in her chest then started beating at a galloping pace. A mix of panic and adrenaline spiked through her, and she scrambled to her hands and knees, crawling as quickly as she could out of the cubbyhole to get away. She didn't make it very far before a large hand clamped around her ankle and pulled hard, flattening her body to the decorative rug. An automatic scream tore from her, and even though her mind knew it was Dean who'd grabbed her, the fantasy was potent enough that the implied danger made her frantic to escape him.

Like a barbaric caveman, he unceremoniously dragged her around to the front of the desk on her stomach, while she desperately reached out to grab hold of something, *anything*, to bring him to a halt so she'd have a better chance to break free. She latched onto the sturdy leg of the desk and when he realized what she'd done, that he couldn't pull her any farther, he released her leg. Her reprieve lasted only seconds before he flipped her onto her back and straddled her waist, pinning her to the floor with the solid strength of his thighs.

Panting for breath, she bucked her hips against him and tried to twist and turn, but he merely smirked at her efforts to dislodge him. Frantically, she pushed at his shoulders, and he caught her flailing hands and secured both of her wrists in one of his hands with his long fingers, leaving his other free to reach into the front pocket of his pants and withdraw a long, thin, plastic zip tie.

He was going to tie her up!

Obviously, he'd planned for this, had known all along that he'd restrain her before fucking her. He stretched her arms high over her head and above the thick wooden leg of the desk then secured the plastic tie around both of her wrists so that there was absolutely no chance left for her to escape. Jerking off her shorts, he tossed them aside and sat back on her thighs so she could no longer kick her legs, either. With her flat on her back, her body in a prone position, she was his prisoner, his captive, and she was completely and utterly helpless to whatever he wanted to do to her.

"You're a little hell-cat, but now I've got you

exactly where I want you," he murmured as he traced a finger from the lace cups of her bra, down the center of her bare stomach, to the elastic edge of her panties.

Excitement and apprehension warred within her while raw tension radiated from him. Moonlight shone through the window behind them, illuminating his gorgeous features and the intense and powerful look in his eyes. Straddling her body and looming above her, he looked so formidable and intimidating and oddly enough it was the scent of his cologne that reassured her, made her feel safe in a potentially terrifying situation . . . until she noticed he'd pulled something else from his pocket that added another level of danger to the fantasy—a tactical and very lethal military knife he kept in his car for emergencies.

With a flick of his thumb, and a soft clicking sound, a frighteningly wicked-sharp blade appeared, glinting in his hand. Shock and hysteria collided inside her, paralyzing her body and vocal chords and making her feel way too vulnerable and defenseless. He didn't move, didn't say a word as he gazed down at her . . . and after a moment she realized that he was waiting for some kind of cue from her before proceeding.

Instinctively, her safe word leapt into her throat, but she swallowed it back, firmly reminding herself that this was Dean, her *husband*, and ultimately she trusted him. This wasn't about pain, but pleasure . . . and she had to admit that fear and desire were a potent mix.

She exhaled the breath she'd been holding, her body's acquiescence all the consent he needed to know he had permission to continue.

"Do *not* move," he commanded gruffly as he slowly, carefully lowered that wicked dagger toward her chest.

He flattened the cold steel blade against her sternum and slid it upward, slipping it between her breasts and beneath the front stitching of her bra. Jill's pulse quickened and she bit her bottom lip, remaining completely motionless as he'd ordered. With one smooth, skillful movement, he sliced away the gusset as easily as if the closure were made from mere threads.

The cups of her bra fell to her sides, exposing her full breasts to the cool air and his heated, hungry gaze. As if mesmerized by the sight, he dragged the blunt side of the knife across her tight nipple, the scraping sensation more erotic than she ever would have believed. Chill bumps rose on her skin, until every part of her tingled with awareness. She moaned softly as he repeated the process on her other stiffened crest before skimming the blunt edge of the knife down her stomach, then to her hip, where he sliced away the flimsy fabric of her panties. He tugged hard on the lace material, tearing it the rest of the way off her body.

"Oh, fuck, *yeah*," he said appreciatively, his voice low and gravelly as he one-handedly closed the knife and set it on the floor a safe distance away. With his knees bracketing her thighs to keep them together, his fingers returned, boldly stroking across her belly before he flattened his palm against her mound and pushed his thumb between the slick folds of her sex, pressing and rubbing against her aching clit. He stroked and teased her, making her writhe and arch toward his touch as he drove her straight toward an explosive orgasm . . . then stopped.

He pulled his hand away, and when she

opened her eyes and looked up at him, he smirked at her.

"You're making this way too easy for me," he said, schooling his expression into something darker and more ruthless as he shoved her legs apart and knelt in between. He removed his shirt, and his hands went to the waistband of his pants as he unbuckled his belt, then lowered the zipper over the massive bulge straining to be released. "*Fight me*, baby girl," he taunted her, once again creating that illusion of danger and distress. "Make me work for it."

He was right. She was being way too passive when this fantasy was all about *resisting* him. With her legs now temporarily freed, she didn't hesitate to plant her foot against his bare chest, and with a swift shove she propelled him backwards. The move was so quick and unexpected that he landed on his ass, but he recovered immediately—and it wasn't as though she could go very far with her hands all trussed up around the leg of the desk.

With a spine-tingling growl he lunged back at her kicking legs, his hands clamping around her calves then gripping her knees. The play of power between them began in earnest as he attempted to spread her legs again, and she did everything she could to dislodge him. He was back to being a rough, savage stranger hell bent on dominating her, and it didn't take long before he was wedged tight between her thighs again, his hips pinning hers to the floor, subduing her body and her struggles.

She was panting from her efforts, her chest rising and falling rapidly as he reached between them, his knuckles grazing across her sex as he freed his erection from his briefs and positioned the head of his cock against her core, where she was so incredibly wet and welcoming.

In the next instant he was rooted eight inches inside her, her shocked gasp and his harsh groan mingling as he moved completely over her, lodging his shaft deeper still. She squirmed beneath the heavy weight of his body and he slid his hands between her back and the carpeted floor, skimming his palms upward until his fingers curved around her shoulders and he had the leverage he needed to hold her in place so he could fuck her *hard*.

His stormy gray eyes bore into hers as he plunged into her tight heat, again and again, his hips pistoning in quick bursts, his thick, rigid cock driving deep with an untamed force that was both raw and primitive. His jaw clenched and his nostril's flared, the intensity of his expression so erotically beautiful as he rode her in a relentless, forceful rhythm that left her breathless and absolutely helpless to do anything but be a vessel to his lust.

She'd unleashed a beast, and this fantasy allowed the man he always tried to keep under control to have free rein with his own dark desires and needs. This fiercely aggressive side to her husband was both frightening and exciting, but she'd wanted this, had *asked* for it, and there was no stopping the rush of pure ecstasy he was hurtling them both towards.

Closing her eyes, she wrapped her legs tight around his waist, submitting to his dominance. Reveling in the full force of his passion, she surrendered to the violent possession of her heart and soul that made her completely and utterly *his*. The wildness of his thrusts escalated as he ground his pubic bone against her clit, adding just the right amount of pressure and friction to send her tumbling over the edge and into a full-bodied orgasm that ripped a hoarse scream from her throat.

She spasmed around his shaft, her inner muscles milking him, and he buried his face against her neck and groaned her name as he came, too. He slammed into her, the searing flood of his release filling her as he climaxed.

Everything about their joining was tumultuous, explosive, and elemental on so many levels. It was physical and emotional bliss in its most exposed state of intimacy.

Lovely, pleasurable aftershocks twitched through her, and she felt his heavy breathing against her neck, stirring her hair. She tried to move her arms to touch him, but the uncomfortable pinch of the plastic tie he'd used stopped her short and made her wince, reminding her that she was still anchored to the leg of the desk.

"Dean . . . I need you to release my hands," she said.

"Oh, shit," he muttered, and immediately lifted off her and reached for the pocket knife he'd put aside. He sliced through the bindings, grabbed her hands, and gently rubbed at the red marks the stiff plastic had left on her wrists. "Jesus, did I hurt you in any way?" he asked, a frantic edge to his voice as he saw the faint welts on her skin. "Dammit, Jill, that's what the safe word is for!"

Clearly, he was worried he'd gone too far in fulfilling her fantasy, that he'd crossed those imaginary boundaries in his own mind that he was so careful not to surpass with her. "I would have used the safe word if I'd needed to, but I didn't," she assured him.

He compressed his lips together, but she saw the tenderness in his gaze. To see his concern, to know how much he cared about her well-being in the aftermath of such a barbaric mating, she fell deeper in love with him in that moment. Despite what had just happened physically, the intimacy, the trust and connection—it was all there, stronger than ever. And that's what mattered the most to her.

"You didn't hurt me in a bad way. I'm fine. Really." The tension gradually eased from his body, and she smiled as he helped her to sit up straight. "But you did ruin one of my favorite bras," she teased lightly.

"You can buy a dozen more," he said unapologetically.

He stood up, and taking her hand in his, he pulled her up onto her feet, too. She swayed slightly from the sudden rush of blood to her head, and he swept her up in his arms and carried her out of the office and down the darkened hall toward their bedroom.

She wrapped her arms around his neck and sighed at his gallant gesture, unable to remember the last time he'd carried her like this—as if she was the most precious thing in the world to him. She cuddled into his chest, absorbing the warmth of his body and inhaling the decadent scent of clean sweat and down-and-dirty sex that clung to his skin.

"I can walk, you know." It was a weak protest, because she loved how safe and secure she felt in his embrace and didn't *really* want him to put her down.

"Really?" He raised a seductive, incredulous brow. "If you can still walk after that, then I didn't fuck you nearly hard enough."

She shivered, not from the cool air on her naked body, but from the veiled and sexy threat in her husband's tone. "Trust me, I'm plenty tender and sore, in the best way possible." The muscles in her thighs ached from his rough and uncivilized thrusts, and she was sensitive in delicate places.

Once he reached their room, he finally set her back on her feet by the side of the bed. Turning the nightstand lamp on its lowest setting, he pulled back the covers and lightly smacked her on the ass. "Get into bed," he ordered.

She crawled up onto the mattress and reclined on her side, watching as Dean quickly stripped off the rest of his clothes. He was so gorgeous, every naked inch of him, and she could stare at him for hours admiring all those masculine lines and contours that made him so virile and impressively male.

He slid onto the bed beside her and pushed her onto her back, half draping his body across hers so that his chest pressed against her breasts and one of his muscular thighs nestled between her legs. He absently threaded his fingers through her hair, spreading the silky strands on the pillow beneath her head, his inquisitive gray eyes searching hers.

"Did it excite you, being chased through the house, knowing I was going to eventually catch you and have my way with you?"

She nodded, her stomach tumbling as she remembered all the conflicting feelings she'd experienced. "It was thrilling and frightening, because the house was so dark and you were so . . . aggressive. And seeing you holding that knife . . . that was incredibly intense," she admitted softly.

"But you didn't use the safe word." His tone was curious as he skimmed a finger down to her breasts and drew lazy, sensual patterns around her hardening nipple.

"Never had a reason to use it," she replied honestly, enjoying the slow hum of desire Dean was once again igniting deep inside her. "I trusted you and knew you'd never hurt me. That's what made the encounter so hot and erotic."

His eyes glowed with masculine satisfaction. "You liked being captured and forced to submit to a stranger." It wasn't a question but rather a statement of fact.

"Only because I knew it was *you*. That made all the difference." She reached up and pushed away a thick lock of hair that had fallen across his forehead. "You far exceeded my expectations in fulfilling my captive fantasy, and now I can scratch that scenario off my sexual bucket list."

"Me, too." He grinned.

She blinked up at him in surprise. "That was a fantasy of yours, too?"

"Yeah, I just didn't know it until we were in the middle of role-playing," he said, giving her nipple a gentle tug she felt all the way down between her thighs. "It gave me quite a rush chasing you in the dark, knowing that once I found you I was going to have my way with you."

His confession fed into that dominant streak he was beginning to whole-heartedly embrace. He liked being the one in control sexually, and she was okay with that—though the idea of being in charge every once in a while did appeal to her, too. "I think I need to return the favor."

Amusement etched his features. "You're going to stalk me, tie me up, and force yourself on me?"

She laughed and shook her head. "No, when you least expect it, I'm going to fulfill *your* fantasy."

He cocked his head, his eyes brightening as

he obviously recalled their Skype conversation a few nights ago. "The one where I take you to a night club and watch you flirt with other men, all the while knowing *I'm* going to be the one to take you home and fuck you?"

"Yep, that fantasy." She smiled, feeling his shaft hardening against her thigh as he thought about how fun and sexy that scenario would be. "You know, I have to admit that I expected your first night back from your business trip to end much differently. Not that I'm complaining about our surprising, and very satisfying, reunion."

He propped his head in his hand, staring down at her, his other hand still caressing her breast. "What did *you* have in mind?"

"The new playroom," she said, unable to prevent the genuine excitement infusing her voice. "Everything was finished today."

"Really?" He looked equally enthusiastic.

She nodded. "Yes. And it's pretty amazing, if I say so myself. I have big plans for you in that playroom, Mr. Noble, but now you're going to have to wait until tomorrow."

His smile immediately turned into a frown,

and he swore beneath his breath. "I need to be at the office for most of the day."

Disappointment curled through her and she actually pouted—something she rarely indulged in. "It's a Saturday, and you've already been gone for ten days." She hated to complain, but she'd thought they'd have the weekend together before he returned to work on Monday.

"I know." He winced, appearing honestly contrite. "Trust me, there's nothing I'd like better than to spend the day with you, especially in this bed or the new playroom, but Mac and I have had this intense training session for our guys scheduled for months."

She sighed. "I understand." And truly, she did. Keeping the men who worked for his security firm in sharp mental and physical shape was a priority for Dean and Mac.

"Tomorrow night, I'm all yours," he promised as he strummed the tips of his fingers along her stomach in a teasing caress and dipped one into her navel, circling lazily.

She'd thought he'd exhausted her physically, but considering the way her body tingled anew, his touch was like carnal magic, effortlessly arousing her all over again.

"I can take you to dinner-"

"I don't want to go out," she said, cutting him off. "I'll make dinner here and make sure you're well fed, because you're going to need a lot of stamina for what I have in mind."

He smirked, a cocky smile that was loaded with that bad boy charm she'd fallen for back in high school. "Stamina doesn't seem to be an issue for me lately. Just being near you makes me hard as granite." He moved his hips, rubbing his impressive erection against her thigh to prove his point. "It doesn't matter that I just fucked you twenty minutes ago. It's like I can't get enough of you."

Her heart raced, that she still had the ability to make her husband of nineteen years crazy with lust and need. All for her. "I like that."

"I think you'll like this even more." He rolled on top of her, settled his hips between her spread thighs and pushed inside of her soft, welcoming body until he was buried to the hilt.

She wrapped her arms around his neck and moaned as he filled her full, then gradually adopted a slow, sensual, in and out rhythm that made everything within her vibrate with renewed desire. "Oh, yes," she said on a delighted sigh. "This is nice. Very nice."

"It's fucking perfect," he agreed, and rubbed his nose alongside hers, the gesture so incredibly sweet and intimate. "God, I missed you," he breathed against her lips, then sealed his mouth over hers for a deep, lush kiss that matched the lazy undulation of his thrusting hips.

While the unrestrained way he'd taken her earlier had been wildly exciting, making love with Dean was absolutely beautiful and sublime. The blissful way his body worshipped hers and the slow, erotic tangle of tongues fed their hunger for one another, and kindled the growing heat between them. There was no mad rush to orgasm, just a drawn out languorous pleasure that was wonderfully relaxing and breath-takingly glorious—and their mutual climax, when it finally sent them both over the edge, was all the more stunning for it.

Afterward, Dean rolled to his back, pulled her against his side, and covered them both with the blanket. Resting her head on his chest so she could listen to the steady beat of his heart, she cuddled into the warmth of his body and released a content sigh. Between the amazing sex and multiple orgasms, Jillian allowed herself to fall into a deep sleep, knowing that she was safe and secure now that her husband was back home where he belonged.

THE PLAYROOM

*D*ean leaned back in his leather chair in his office at home and took a deep swallow of Scotch, trying like hell to be patient while he waited for Jillian to finish cleaning up the kitchen after the dinner she'd made. Time seemed to drag by, or maybe he was just anxious to move on to the next phase of their evening and therefore every minute seemed like an eternity.

For a man who prided himself on his restraint and control, he had to admit he was curious as hell about the playroom his newly adventurous wife had put together for the two of them to enjoy. Just imagining what she intended to do to him tonight, and what those "big plans" she'd promised entailed, had him intrigued and already half hard with anticipation.

He smiled to himself as he swirled the amber liquid in the cut crystal glass. He loved the changes in Jillian, and her newfound confidence and sensuality, along with her openness to try all sorts of exciting and kinky things, definitely blew him away. Over the past few weeks they'd grown closer, both emotionally and physically, and while he'd always desired Jillian, his need for her was now like a living, breathing thing . . . consuming his idle thoughts and bringing out a possessive side to him that she seemed to like, a lot. Last night's stranger/captive fantasy had confirmed as much, and fulfilling that scenario for her had been hot as hell for him, as well.

"Are you ready to see the playroom?"

Dean had been so lost in his thoughts he hadn't heard Jillian step into the office, and that was saying something considering how alert he normally was. She stood just inside the door, wearing a lavender summer dress with a row of pearl buttons down the front, and no shoes on her bare feet. Her long hair was pulled into a ponytail, her make-up was minimal, and even at thirty-seven she looked as young and fresh-faced as the sweet, innocent girl she'd been when he'd dated her in high school.

She'd stolen his heart way back then, and he could easily say she *still* owned him, body and soul. Even after nineteen years of marriage.

He finished the last of his Scotch, set the empty glass on his desk, then stood up and walked toward Jillian. "I've been ready since the moment I got home."

A sultry smile, filled with all sorts of erotic promises, curved her full lips. "Anticipation is a very powerful thing."

The low purr of her voice was like a stroke straight to his dick, tenting the front of his jeans. When he reached her, she splayed a hand to his chest and pushed him back a few steps, until he was pressed against the wall—quickly establishing who was going to be in control tonight. She smoothed her palm up around to the back of his neck, then pulled his head down to hers until their lips meshed and the silky heat of her tongue slipped inside his mouth to tangle with his.

He let her set the pace of the kiss, a slow, deep seduction that was better and more decadent than any after-dinner-dessert he'd ever tasted. Settling his hands at her hips, he pulled her in close, aligning their bodies in all the right places and pressing the thick length of his erection against the notch between her thighs.

She exhaled a soft, dreamy "mmmm," and ended the too brief kiss. She looked up into his eyes, the irises dark with desire. "I've been thinking about you all day long, and all the things I'm going to do with you in the playroom," she whispered as she grabbed one of his hands and slipped it beneath the hem of her dress, guiding his flattened palm up her thigh while watching his expression. "It's been so hard resisting the urge not to touch myself and ease the throbbing ache, because I'm saving it all for you."

When they reached the barrier of her panties, she pushed his fingers beneath the elastic edge, and *oh, fuck*, she was absolutely drenched, her cunt so soft and silky it made

ERIKA WILDE

his entire body pound with the need to give her the pleasure she'd denied herself all day long.

She moved her lips up to his ear, her warm breath caressing his throat on the way. "I can't wait to feel your tongue right here," she said, pressing two of his fingers against her clit before sliding them lower, until the blunt tips entered her body a few tantalizing inches. "And your cock deep inside me *here*."

Beyond aroused by his wife's explicit words and brazen attitude, a ragged groan rumbled in his chest. "I'm more than happy to oblige you, right here and now," he said, meaning it.

She shook her head and pulled his hand from beneath her dress. "As tempting as your offer is, I think tonight it's *your* turn to learn all about patience and restraint."

Those damning words, the same ones he'd used on her the night he'd taken her to dinner and spent the entire evening tormenting her sexually, came back to taunt him now. The tables were turned, and she was going to make him suffer—and he was totally up for the challenge.

"I want to hear you beg tonight," she said,

168

the notion of him at her total mercy obviously appealing to her in a big way.

Amusement coursed through him, because he'd never in his life begged for anything. "You can certainly try your best," he replied, invoking a deliberate dare in his voice.

She laughed, the sound filled with pure, female determination. "Oh, you have no idea what my *best* is, but you're about to find out."

She took his hand and led him out of his office and down the hallway, just past the kitchen to the door that led to their basement. It looked like any other door in the house— white and inset with panels—except there was a small white box mounted beside the door frame. She pushed the cover up, revealing a key pad beneath, and punched in a series of numbers that unlocked the door with a soft "click".

She flashed him a sassy grin. "The code to release the lock is our wedding anniversary. Month, day, and year. If you don't remember the date, you don't deserve to gain access to our playroom," she teased him.

He chuckled. "It's a date I'll never forget."

"Good. I decided to put a lock on the door

because I didn't want the boys, or anyone else, to accidentally find our little den of iniquity."

He appreciated her foresight and caution because he couldn't imagine having to explain their *playroom* to their grown-up sons or guests.

She opened the door and flicked a switch on the wall inside, and a row of elegant antique sconces topped with red crystal globes lit a pathway down the flight of stairs, giving the impression that they were entering a secret chamber. The scent of vanilla and cinnamon beckoned, and when they finally reached the cool interior of the basement, Dean was blown away by what greeted him—and how much she'd accomplished in the time he'd been away on his business trip.

The original stark white walls had been painted a warm shade of beige to match the new plush carpeting, but the main color scheme was a deep, dark, amethyst. The carved wooden bed she'd bought was draped with purple silk sheets—no comforter since he didn't think they'd be sleeping much on that mattress—as were the cases on the pillows. Splashes of red throughout the room offset all the purple, including the abstract paintings and the sconces on the walls that provided the room with a dim glow of red that was incredibly erotic—as were all the smoky mirrors hanging in strategic places that would make them voyeurs to each other's pleasure.

She'd transformed the spacious underground room into a seductive haven that both stunned and aroused him.

"Wow," he said, trying to take it all in. "This playroom is beyond anything I thought it would be."

She smiled, clearly proud of her efforts. "I take it you like it?"

He nodded. "Oh, yeah."

"Well, this is just a start," she said, caressing her slender fingers over the silk bed-sheet in a way that made him eager to feel her hands on *him*. "As you can see, there's plenty of space down here to add other things as we like."

A few stimulating items sprang to mind, like the addition of a sex swing or wall restraints, but for now, he could easily make do with the basics.

She strolled toward him then brushed a soft kiss along his cheek. "Go ahead and look around while I change into something more . . . *appropriate*."

He watched her walk into the bathroom she'd also redecorated in the same alluring shade of purple, more than a little tempted to follow her inside and just take her right there on the sink, or in the shower, or up against the wall. But he was too intrigued to discover what she deemed *appropriate* for this situation to give into that urge.

She closed the door, leaving him alone to explore their new playroom. He stepped up to the bed—the one she'd purchased from a local artisan who commissioned erotic furniture—and skimmed a hand down one of the substantial, hand carved posts. The frame itself was sturdy, with thick, individual slats running along the lower portion of the headboard, perfect to withstand the tug and pull of restraints, while the top piece was inlaid with those same smoky mirrors she'd placed throughout the room.

He glanced up, catching sight of his image in the reflective glass in the overhead canopy, and grinned as he imagined watching their bodies writhing on the bed as he fucked Jillian.

Very nice.

Exhaling a deep breath, he continued his tour, curious to see what was inside the matching armoire positioned in one corner near the bed. He opened the double doors and found a flat-screen TV and a DVD player just in case they wanted to watch some adult entertainment as foreplay—or maybe they'd make their own sex tape, he mused. The drawers below were filled with the few basic sex toys they'd played with prior to Jillian's request to be more adventurous, and there was plenty of space to store many more new, kinkier devices.

He closed the armoire doors and approached the hand-blown, decorative glass vase that Jillian had shown him that night they'd Skyped. The one she'd bought for the two of them to fill with their personal fantasies so that when they wanted inspiration or the element of surprise they could blindly pick one and act out the proposed scene. He noticed that there were already two folded pieces of paper inside the wide rimmed vase, and he didn't hesitate to jot down his own wicked suggestion with the pen and small pad of paper she'd left right next to the vase. When he was done, he folded the note into a neat square then dropped it into the vase just as he heard the bathroom door open behind him.

He turned around, took one look at Jillian's sexy dominatrix outfit, with her hair soft and disheveled around her face and shoulders, and felt as though he'd been delivered a swift punch to the solar plexus—leaving him dazed and unable to speak.

He'd seen his wife in provocative lingerie dozens of times, but nothing like *this*. A tight red satin and lace corset hugged her midsection, pushing her voluptuous breasts up so that they nearly spilled from the confines of the bustier. The one-piece garment cinched in at the waist and flared out at her hips, giving her a lush, curvaceous centerfold figure. Matching *barely there* panties covered her mound, while sheer red stockings encased her long, slender legs, all the way down to a pair of red stilettos with a five-inch heel.

She stood with her feet braced apart, and it was the interesting object she held in her hands that eventually captured his undivided attention—a black leather riding crop that she was casually smacking against her palm. Everything about her demeanor was commanding and assertive, unnervingly so for a man who preferred the upper hand in the bedroom, yet he was completely captivated by this bold and confident woman before him.

Lust twisted through him and his cock rose to the occasion. He was so screwed, in more ways than one. "Oh, fuck me," he muttered, finally able to speak.

A triumphant smile tipped the corner of her mouth as she strolled toward him, closing the distance between them. "If you're a good boy, maybe I will," she said, caressing the leather tip of the crop down the burgeoning seam of his jeans.

Anticipation and excitement mingled through him, along with a healthy dose of respect for that crop she was wielding. "And if I'm bad?" he dared to ask.

"Corporal punishment, of course." She very lightly tapped the sturdy flap against the swell of his erection to give him a taste of said punishment, and damn if his dick didn't harden even more.

She circled around him, dragging the crop along his ass, his thighs, keeping him tense and on edge as to where she might smack next. Much to his relief, and maybe a bit of disappointment, she didn't use it on him again.

Standing in front of him, she met his gaze, a delightful mix of satisfaction and heat brightening her beautiful green/gold eyes. "Tonight, you're all mine, to do with as I desire," she instructed, clearly enjoying her more dominant facade. "You're my slave, and you'll address me as *mistress*. You'll do as you're told or suffer the consequences, understand, *slave?*" She emphasized the request with another firm slap of the crop against her palm.

God, she was so freaking hot that he had to curb the impulse to pounce on her, pin her to the floor, and show her all about *consequences*. Instead, he assumed the role she asked of him and replied accordingly. "Yes . . . *mistress*."

"Although, if things get too intense, you can use the safe word we've established." Her too sweet voice held just a trace of provocation.

He smirked, knowing there wasn't anything she could do to him to make him cry uncle. However . . . "I have a feeling you'll be making me *beg* for mercy before the night is through." Not use it as a safe word.

"Oh, you have no idea, slave." A secretive smile curved her lips. "Now take off all your clothes."

He toed off his shoes first and removed his socks, then pulled his shirt over his head and let it drop to the floor while she watched. He stripped off his jeans and boxer briefs together and caught her staring at his already raging erection. She licked her lips, and he swallowed a groan, wondering for the first time if he'd truly be able to withstand whatever she planned to do to him. If he had the ability to be obedient and complacent, when those characteristics went against every fiber of his alpha-male being.

"Very nice," she murmured appreciatively as her eat-him-up gaze roamed his naked, aroused body. "Get on the bed and lie on your back," she ordered in a curt tone.

He hesitated for second, struggling against the more dominating emotions swirling inside him, then turned toward the bed—and sucked in a quick breath as she snapped the leather crop against his bare ass, which left a stinging, burning sensation in its wake that actually made his cock twitch, shocking him with the knowledge that he was clearly *aroused*.

Stunned, he stopped mid-movement and glanced over his shoulder at Jillian, raising an incredulous, *what-the-fuck* brow. What the hell had he done to instigate *that*?

In return, she arched a haughty brow right back at him and swatted his other cheek, just to show him who was in command. "Do as I say the first time, slave. Any disobedience will earn you the wrath of this crop in much more tender places."

She was enjoying herself, and the power she wielded, *way* too much. Unwilling to test her threat, he climbed up onto the mattress and positioned himself on his back, as she'd instructed. She walked over to the armoire and came back a few seconds later with restraints.

"Hands above your head," she said.

He lifted his arms, and one by one she secured each of his wrists to the slatted part of the headboard with a strip of soft velvet rope she must have purchased while he'd been gone. Her knots were loose so as not to chafe his skin, but what she didn't realize was that her bindings were flimsy enough that one good hard tug would release him. But for as easy as it would be for him to escape, he wasn't about to risk her displeasure when the nearest target for her crop was his straining-at-attention cock.

She casually strolled along the side of the bed, trailing the leather tip of the crop along his body in a soft, seductive caress that was a complete contradiction to the singe of pain he knew that little whip could inflict on a moment's notice. Over his chest, across his taut belly, and down his thigh she stroked, until she finally reached the foot of the mattress.

"Spread your legs," she directed as she tapped the inside of his knees with the crop before sliding it all the way up to his balls.

Eyeing just how close that damn crop was to his man parts, he quickly obeyed, planting his feet wide apart.

She moved up onto the bed and settled on her knees in the space he'd just made for her, then reached out and gripped his erection in her hand. Squeezing the hard column of flesh tightly with her fingers, she rubbed her thumb over the drop of pre-cum beaded on the sensitive head and smeared it down his shaft. His hips bucked in response to her ministrations, and she smiled up at him like a tempting Cheshire cat.

"Would you like me to suck your cock?" she asked huskily.

"Oh, hell yeah," he said, the eager words slipping out before he could stop them.

She gave him a mock frown and punished his impudence with three consecutive swats to the inside of his thigh, where the skin was most tender. *Fuck.* His entire body jerked involuntarily, but what started out as shocking bites of discomfort gradually gave way to a tingling sensation that added to his already aroused state.

"Where are your manners, slave?" she asked, scolding him for being so rude, though she couldn't completely hide the humor in her gaze. Clearly, she liked tormenting him.

"Yes, *please*, mistress," he said politely.

"That's much better," she said, caressing her cool fingers over the hot spot she'd created on his thigh, her touch both soothing and highly stimulating. "I'm going to suck your cock, but you may not come. Do you understand?"

The wicked gleam in her eyes didn't bode

well for him, but what man refused an offered blow job? Not climaxing was a matter of mind over matter . . . and he prided himself on his control in intense situations. This would be no different. He could enjoy the pleasure of Jillian giving him head, without going off like an inexperienced teenaged boy.

He nodded his agreement, and she bent over him. The moment her warm mouth enveloped his dick his pep talk disintegrated into smoke, because it was clear from the get-go that she intended to test his limits. Her tongue swirled along the length of his thick shaft as she took him deep, until the tumescent crown pressed against the back of her throat and he was completely engulfed in all that silky, wet heat. She made a sweet, hungry, "mmm" sound that rippled along his cock, then slowly withdrew, sucking on him as if he were a cherry flavored popsicle on a scorching-hot summer day and she needed every bit of moisture she could draw from him. His blood thrummed in his veins as she devoured him, again and again, the tight circle of her fingers pumping his erection while her sinful mouth and velvet tongue drove him to the brink of insanity.

His breathing turned harsh as he valiantly tried to maintain a grip on the orgasm threatening to erupt. Desperately needing to distract himself, he glanced up at the mirrored canopy above the bed, which added a whole new erotic element to the situation. He was tied down, sprawled naked on the bed, with Jillian positioned on her knees between his legs while her head bobbed up and down as she sucked his cock. The tumble of her dark hair and the bright red corset were a vivid contrast to her creamy skin, and he couldn't tear his gaze away from her heart shaped ass perched high in the air, wiggling back and forth in a way that told him she was rubbing her own thighs together to ease the ache in between.

The visual and physical stimulation overwhelmed him. He was her slave, all right. A slave to her passion, her hunger, her heart and soul. This woman, *his wife*, owned every single piece of him. Driving need pounded at him, and he decided whatever punishment she doled out for his insubordination would be well worth the unparalleled ecstasy he was about to experience.

His hips thrust of their own accord to the rhythm she'd set, forcing him deeper as he mindlessly fucked her mouth. Release beckoned, and all he could do was feel the incredible sensations building within him, tightening his belly and simmering in his balls until he couldn't hold back any longer.

His eyes rolled back, his hands curled into fists, and his entire body arched as his orgasm slammed through him. He roared like a savage warrior as he came in a hard, throbbing rush, and she took all of him, sucking every bit of essence from his cock until he had nothing left to give.

Utterly wasted, he went slack on the mattress, his chest heaving as he tried to regain his equilibrium, which was extremely difficult to do with Jillian trailing hot, open-mouthed kisses over his stomach, then higher. She moved up and over him, and he pried his eyes back open just as she straddled his chest then lifted up on her knees, only inches away from his face, giving him a clear view of the crotch of her panties. The silky material was soaked through, and the scent of her own need and desire filled his senses, making his limp cock stir to life again.

God, he was so fucking easy when it came to her.

"I really should punish you for coming when I specifically told you not to, but I'll give you the chance to redeem yourself by returning the favor," she said meaningfully, and released the clever Velcro strips at the sides of her panties so she didn't have to slide them down her legs. She tossed the fabric aside and dipped her fingers through her wet, gleaming pussy, spreading the smooth, bare lips of her sex apart so he could see *everything.*

Christ, she was absolutely *killing* him.

"Look what sucking you off does to me," she said teased huskily.

Dean couldn't have looked away, even if someone were holding a gun to his head while ordering him to do so. She touched herself, gathering all that honeyed heat onto one of her fingers before spreading that slick moisture along his bottom lip.

"Taste me," she commanded, and pushed her finger into his mouth.

Greedily, he sucked the tip, then the entire length, the heady, exotic flavor of her dancing on his tongue. Too soon for his liking, she withdrew her finger, her lips curving into a vixen-like smile.

"Would you like more?" she asked.

"Yes, please," he replied, not giving a damn how enthusiastic he sounded.

Satisfied with his response, she moved higher, adjusting her knees on either side of his head so that she was poised right above his mouth, but instead of immediately giving her what she wanted, he decided to impart the only bit of control he had over the situation.

Turning his head, he nuzzled her inner thigh, breathing a hot rush of air over that tender, sensitive skin that made her shiver and her anticipation rise. "Tell me what you want, mistress," he murmured, making *her* ask for the pleasure she craved.

Keeping in character with her dominant behavior, she clutched a fistful of his hair and turned his head, positioning his mouth against her sex. "Lick me, slave."

Her assertive demeanor and words fueled his excitement and he didn't hesitate to obey.

He stroked his tongue along her slit in a series of long, leisurely laps that made her breath hitch in her throat and her back arch.

"Suck my clit," she rasped.

He closed his lips around that bead of flesh, flicked his tongue over the hardened nub, and suckled, softly at first, then increasingly harder, deeper.

A soft, ragged moan escaped her, and her legs trembled. "Fuck me with your tongue."

Her explicit demand shot through him like a hot poker, and he thrust his tongue inside her core, again and again, until she began the slow, desperate grind of her pussy against his open mouth. He glanced up the length of her body, expecting to find her eyes on him, but instead her heavy-lidded gaze was transfixed on the mirrors on the headboard that reflected back on the two of them, her face flushed and her lips parted as she stared in fascination at the erotic image of him going down on her.

"Oh, God," she gasped helplessly, her voice intoxicated with desire and lust. "Make me come. *Now.*"

She was soft, hot, and delicious, and he could eat her for hours, but her command ruled him, and he gave her what she wanted. He doubled his efforts—licking, feasting, and sliding his tongue over every inch of her until her thighs tightened around his head and the first quake of her climax began then completely overtook her. She went wild, crying out as she bucked and writhed and flooded his mouth with the luscious nectar of her orgasm.

When the last of her tremors faded away, she scooted down, sat astride his stomach, and collapsed against his chest in a boneless heap. She buried her face against his neck, her breathing erratic, and he gave her a few moments to regain her strength while he wallowed in the egotistical male gratification of her complete and utter satisfaction that he was solely responsible for.

"Are you okay?" he asked after a while.

She lifted her head and he didn't miss the tempting spark in her eyes that promised even more debauchery. "I'm perfect, but far from done with you."

Thank God, because he was rock hard and raring to go again, his cock one huge, monumental, pulsing ache between his thighs. He thought for sure she'd release his hands, but she kept him tethered to the headboard as she moved off the bed and looked for something in one of the armoire drawers.

He couldn't begin to imagine what more she had planned, but it didn't take long to find out. She returned, and he groaned as her fingers fondled his straining dick then frowned when he felt an odd pressure tighten around the base of his penis. Curious to see exactly what she was doing, he raised his head and glanced down to find that Jillian had secured some kind of device to his man parts that he assumed was a cock ring, since they'd never used one before. Already, he could feel the restriction of blood flow, increasing the size and thickness of his erection.

"What the hell?" he muttered, unsure how he felt about having his cock manacled.

She gave him a smug smile, letting him know she had him by the balls in more ways than one. "Obviously, you can't be trusted not to come, so this cock ring will keep you good and hard until I'm ready to let you orgasm again."

Holy shit. He watched as she straddled his hips then slowly lowered herself onto his burgeoning shaft, her body seemingly lique-fying around him like molten fire until he was seated to the hilt inside her. She didn't move right away, but instead unhooked the front of her corset, all the way down to the bottom. Once the lingerie came undone, she tossed the contraption to the floor, leaving her gloriously naked except for her stockings and stilettos.

Lust and desire flushed her skin an enticing shade of pink, and the sight of her full breasts and erect nipples made his mouth salivate for a taste. Tipping her head back so that her hair cascaded down her spine, she rocked against him, and he closed his eyes and instinctively thrust upward to match the movements of her body, pushing and sliding into the tight clasp of her sheath.

The sharp, stinging snap against his nipple electrified his nerve endings, a swift reminder that he was still under her command, and his hands yanked reflexively on his restraints. He bit back a string of curse words while he waited for the pain to recede. Damn, he'd forgotten about the crop!

From her position on top of his cock, Jillian arched a brow down at him as she tapped the leather tip against his stomach. "Did I say that you could fuck me?"

She sounded so imperious, every inch the mistress to his slave, and even though he wanted to rebel and take charge, he let her indulge the rest of her fantasy. For now.

"No, mistress," he replied, forcing a humble, obedient note to his voice for the sake of the illusion of power she'd created between them. And that's all it was—an illusion—because he just realized that those velvet ropes she'd secured around his wrists were gradually coming undone. At any point, he had the ability to turn the tables on his wife . . . but not just yet. He was enjoying this playful and sexually confident side of Jillian way too much to steal her thunder.

"This pleasure is for me, not you," she said as he lowered her hand down to where their bodies were joined, her fingers fiddling with the cock ring circling the base of his shaft. "Do *not* move. All you get to do for now is watch."

A second later, the device began to buzz, making him realize that this toy had a built-in vibrator. His entire cock began to hum, the warm, tingling sensation adding to his already sensitized dick, yet the rubber ring kept any kind of orgasm at bay, just as she'd intended. Curbing the impulse to thrust took monumental effort, especially when she started riding his cock in a slow, sensual, rocking motion that added yet another element of heat and friction to the mix.

With a delightful sigh, she cupped her full breasts in her hands and rolled the taut nipples between her fingers, her body moving fluidly, gracefully, on top of his erection. She pressed down, letting the vibrator make contact with her clitoris, then dropped her head back and moaned as she lifted back up again, all the way to the plump head of his cock before seating herself again and grinding her pussy against the thrumming implement.

He watched everything in abject fascination – the way her body undulated against his in an erotic lap dance, the way her hands caressed her breasts, and the radiant look of bliss transforming her beautiful features as she rocked harder, faster, on top of him in shameless abandon.

Who *was* this bewitching woman? She was his *wife*, he thought with awe. His gorgeous, seductive, wildly uninhibited wife, and he loved being a spectator to this emerging, sexually confident side of her personality.

She started to pant, and he knew she was getting close to coming, like he was aching to do, but couldn't because she had him by the balls, literally. All he could do was *feel* . . . the clasp of her pussy, the wet, suctioning heat, the mind-blowing friction. The cock ring had him full to bursting and prolonged the agonizing pleasure, tempting and teasing him with the promise of a release of Herculean proportions once the contraption was removed.

But it was her orgasm that came first, and she cried out as she gyrated against the vibrator, her entire body shuddering above him while inner contractions pulsed around his enormous erection. The muscles in Dean's abdomen tightened, and he gritted his teeth until he couldn't take the torment any longer and his control snapped.

He tugged on his flimsy restraints, once, twice, *hard*, and the velvet ropes unraveled, freeing him. In one smooth move, he flipped Jillian onto her back, and she gasped in shock as he loomed over her, her wide eyes taking in his ferocious expression. She'd had her fun, and now it was time to remind her who was truly in charge.

He pinned her beneath him, spreading his knees wide to force her legs apart while the tip of his cock pressed against her soft, wet opening. "Take off the goddamn cock ring so I can fuck you the way I *need* to," he growled, a note of desperation to his voice. "The way I've been *dying* to."

An unexpected smile touched her lips and her eyes shimmered playfully. "Are you *begging?*" she asked oh-so-sweetly.

It was more of a *demand*, but he wasn't about to split hairs when the end result would be the same, so he gave her what she wanted to hear. "Yes, I'm begging."

Her radiant expression turned triumphant, and she reached between them and removed the tight rubber band encircling his shaft. The release of pressure was so immense he groaned, but lust and need still pounded through him, and with a hard, driving thrust he planted himself balls deep inside her. He almost lost it the moment her soft, heated depths sheathed his too sensitive cock, and he knew he wasn't going to last long at all.

He surged into her, over and over, and she wrapped her long legs around his waist, locking her stilettos at the base of his spine and tipping her hips for better, deeper penetration. She arched into him, her nails digging against his back, marking him, and he felt the electrified scraping sensation all the way down to his groin. She breathed into his ear then sucked on a patch of skin on his neck, sending him straight into orbit.

Heat pulsed from his balls to the tip of his cock as his orgasm blasted through him, ripping a hoarse, primitive, beastly howl from his chest. The pleasure was so intense, so powerful, that he could have sworn he'd passed out as he collapsed on top of her.

His senses returned sometime later at the feel of Jillian stroking her fingers up and down the slope of his back. Lifting his head took effort, but he managed to look down at his wife's very gleeful expression and bright cheerful eyes that were filled with way too much mirth.

"You actually *begged*," she said, and laughed huskily.

He grinned at her, letting her have her moment of sheer delight before letting her know that while she might have won this battle, he intended to win the war. "Just remember, sweetheart. Paybacks are hell."

THE TEMPTATION

A DIARY ENTRY

diary entry from Jillian Noble:

The playroom was a huge success, more so than I ever could have predicted, and playing the role of dominatrix to my sexy husband was incredibly fun and thrilling. He might have been uncomfortable at first being tied down with me in charge, but it didn't take Dean long to get into the fantasy. Last night was erotic, exciting, adventurous, and all the things I hoped it would be.

Who would have thought that hot sex and fulfilling fantasies would not only awaken our deepest, most illicit passions, but also bring us closer as a couple? The physical pleasure between us is undeniable, and the emotional intimacy is only making our marriage stronger on every level. I'm learning that unconditional trust is the key to satisfying every single one of our desires, and there isn't anything I wouldn't do to increase Dean's pleasure, and my own.

SWEET REVENGE

I have a few errands to take care of. I'll be back in a few hours and when I return I expect you to be ready to do exactly as I say.

Dean's parting words earlier that Sunday afternoon played through Jillian's mind long after he'd gone, wreaking havoc with her ability to focus on anything that required concentration because she couldn't stop speculating about what those *errands* might entail. Judging by the wicked grin he'd given her as he'd left, she was fairly certain her husband had come up with a fitting retribution as payback to making him her slave last night in their new playroom.

Her stomach tumbled at the thought. Knowing Dean, and how much he was enjoying the erotic games they were now engaging in, she prepared herself to expect the unexpected. She'd been married to Dean for nineteen years and knew him better than anyone else on a soul deep level, but when it came to sexual fantasies and kinks she was discovering that her husband had a penchant for bondage and discipline, which tied directly into that dominant streak he'd suppressed for their entire marriage . . . until she'd given him permission to explore that assertive side to his personality in the parameters of their bedroom.

Or in this case, the playroom.

In an attempt to make the time pass faster, and to keep her occupied until Dean returned, she headed into the kitchen and baked a couple dozen sugar cookies then put together two separate care packages to send to each of her sons—one who was away at college, and the other in the Navy. Just as she finished washing the dirty dishes she heard the rolling garage door open then close again. She turned around as Dean entered the kitchen, carrying a large black gift bag she instantly recognized as belonging to Sugar and Spice, the adult boutique where she'd purchased her dominatrix outfit and the cock ring she'd used on her husband just last night.

While the outside packaging was discreet, there was no doubt that the items tucked inside the bag—the items Dean had selected and bought—were anything but demure or straight-laced.

A familiar sense of anticipation shimmied through her, spiraling through her stomach and settling between her thighs as he closed the distance between them. "I see you went shopping," she said, trying not to sound too enthusiastic.

"I did." Much too casually, he set the bag on the counter next to where she was standing, and smiled at her. "I stopped by Sugar and Spice and picked up a few things for you, and me. Your friend, Raina, was very helpful with her suggestions about what you might enjoy the most."

His voice was husky and confident, and

Jillian's pulse skipped a beat. Raina knew plenty of her fantasies, and while she knew her friend wouldn't spill her secrets, that didn't mean Raina wouldn't possibly direct Dean toward some of the more risqué items in her adult boutique that had intrigued Jillian.

"What did you buy?" Dying to peek inside his bag of tricks, she stood up on tip-toe and skimmed her fingers along the top edge, hoping to get a glimpse of what was inside.

He playfully smacked her hand away. "That's for me to know, and for *you* to find out. Eventually. I wouldn't want to spoil the element of surprise. Suffice it to say, I think you'll enjoy tonight's payback."

Leaving the bag on the counter to taunt her, he turned and headed toward the refrigerator. He opened the door, peered inside, and pulled out the bottle of whipped cream flavored Vodka she kept chilled for an occasional muddled strawberry martini. The sweetly infused alcohol made the drink taste like a strawberry shortcake dessert with a slight kick.

He grabbed a small cut crystal tumbler from her china hutch then returned, setting the glass on the counter and filling it with an inch of the clear liquor.

"Since when do you drink my girly vodka?" she asked curiously, especially when his tastes always ran toward smoky, expensive scotch.

"I don't," he said as he recapped the bottle. "This is for you."

"Me?" She frowned, not understanding why he felt the need to pour her a drink.

"Just one shot of vodka," he murmured, a bad boy glint in his eyes as he moved to stand in front of her, just inches away. "I want you relaxed and accommodating for what I have in mind."

Amusement warred with the thrum of arousal already sifting through her veins. "Don't you mean you want me obedient and submissive?" she retorted with way too much sass.

"Oh, you'll be those things, too," he assured her in a lazy, sexy drawl as he touched the rim of the glass to her lips and slowly, but firmly, tipped it upward. "Bottoms up, baby girl."

Ensnared by his mesmerizing gaze, she let him pour the flavored vodka into her mouth.

The liquid was initially cold and sweet against her tongue then grew hot, generating a burning trail of arousing heat down her throat as she swallowed. The alcohol settled into her stomach like a warm ball of fire and gradually spread outward, toward her extremities.

The one shot wasn't enough to get her drunk or dull her senses. Quite the opposite, actually. Her nerve endings seemed to tingle as the liquor worked its way through her system, subtly stimulating every one of her female erogenous zones. Definitely intoxicating, in a purely sensuous way.

"Good girl," he praised, and placed the empty glass in the sink behind her.

Sliding a warm hand behind her neck, he lowered his mouth to hers. His lips were initially soft then grew more demanding as he opened wider and deepened the kiss. He stepped closer, aggressively pressing her back against the counter with the sheer strength of his body aligned to hers.

He felt so good—the crush of his chest against her breasts, the thick length of his cock nestled at the crux of her thighs, and the hand

he'd skimmed down over her jean-clad bottom
that was now kneading her butt. His long
fingers followed the seam running down her
ass until he reached her cleft. He rubbed her
through the denim, while seducing her mouth
with his deep, luxurious, make-out kisses—the
kind that made a woman willingly drop her
panties and spread her legs because she wanted
to feel that skillful mouth elsewhere.

She moaned against Dean's damp lips, her
hips rocking into his firm, knowing touch,
increasing the pressure and friction against her
clit. Just when she was on the verge of unraveling, he moved his hand back up to her waist
and lifted his mouth from hers.

Her fingers tightened on his shirt as she
tried to contain her whimper of disappointment, but failed.

Staring down at her upturned face, he
licked his lips slowly, sensually. "You taste like
sugar cookies and whipped cream," he
murmured huskily as he dipped his head and
nibbled his way up the side of her neck. "I want
to eat you up."

"Yes, please," she said, her voice breathless.

At this rate, she didn't even care if they made it to the playroom. She was already aching, pulsing with the need for him to finish what he'd just started.

He chuckled against her ear. "Already begging. You're so easy."

And apparently, completely shameless as well. "I'll be as easy as you want, so long as you make me come." *Preferably, right now.*

He drew back, a dark brow arched in feigned surprise. "Don't I always?"

"*Eventually*, yes." She sounded perturbed, even to her own ears.

The hand at her hip skimmed beneath her T-shirt, his warm fingers feathering up her abdomen until his large palm engulfed one of her breasts and squeezed hard, making her wish she wasn't wearing a bra. "This was just a warm-up, a little tease of what to expect once I have you in the playroom."

She remembered how she'd withheld his orgasms, how she'd made him delirious with the need to come before allowing him that pleasure, and wondered if he'd make her suffer the same fate—one she had mixed feelings about. "Are you going to keep me on edge all night?"

"No, I'm not going to torture you like you did me," he said, though she wasn't certain she believed him. "You'll be happy to know that I plan to make you come, and often . . . with my fingers, with my mouth, with my cock, and possibly a few other ways."

Her imagination ran wild as to what those *other ways* might entail, because she'd yet to find out what he'd bought today at Sugar and Spice.

He removed his hand from her breast, leaving her nipples tight and aching, just like the rest of her body. "I'm feeling very generous—"

"And obviously very presumptuous about your ability to make me come so many times in one night," she goaded, letting her sexual frustration get the best of her.

"Challenge accepted, baby girl." An abundance of humor and self-assurance laced his deep, seductive voice. "Let's see how many orgasms I can wring out of you tonight, how many different ways I can make you come. But just know this . . . every one of those orgasms is going to be on *my* terms, not yours."

Jillian's heart raced, because she knew just how well her husband toed the fine line between pleasure and pain, and how much he enjoyed inflicting both sensations. How he so effortlessly brought her to the precipice and kept her there until she was pleading for release.

But it was the smug look on his face right now that prompted her to be a little reckless with her words, even though she knew better than to provoke him when he clearly had the upper hand tonight. Then again, maybe it was the shot of vodka that was making her so brazen, and her tongue so loose.

"Don't disappoint me," she retorted impudently.

He braced his hands on the counter on either side of her waist and leaned in close, his expression dark and dangerous enough to make her question her decision to be so impulsive and bold. "I'm thinking I should have bought a ball gag at Sugar and Spice for your smart mouth," he said in a calm tone that belied the flash of threat in his gaze. "Then again, I'm all about improvising if I need to, so you'd better think twice about being so defiant."

Shock rippled through her. "You wouldn't dare gag me!"

He lifted a hand and slid the pad of his thumb across her lower lip, looking much too intrigued by the idea. "Oh, I definitely *would* dare, so don't tempt me."

Picking up the black bag he'd left on the counter, he stepped away from her. "I want you in the playroom in ten minutes," he ordered succinctly. "Get undressed and put on your red silk robe. I want you completely naked underneath. Don't make me wait."

With that, he turned and walked away. Not wanting to waste any time, she went to the master bedroom and stripped off her clothes then covered up with the crimson-red silk robe Dean had indicated. The cool, smooth material slid along her bare skin like a lover's caress, and her nipples tightened against the luxurious fabric, as if anticipating the touch of Dean's fingers, the wet heat of his mouth. *Soon.*

Shivering at the decadent thought, she

cinched the silk sash around her waist in a secure knot then ruffled her fingers through her unbound hair and added a bit of cherry Chapstick to her lips to keep them soft and moist. Not wanting to be late, she headed to the playroom, punched in the security code to unlock the door to their newly furnished basement, and made her way down the carpeted stairs.

A sense of pride filled her at how well her decorating ideas had come together and just how erotic this room had become with its deep, dark purple hues and smoky mirrors—definitely a sinful escape from the simplicity of their master bedroom and what had become a very predictable sex life. This was a place where they could shed inhibitions and do or be anything they wanted.

Last night, she'd indulged in a sexy, fun, dominatrix fantasy that had been immensely satisfying for her, but this evening was all about Dean's desires. And *holy crap*, right now her gorgeous husband was standing at the foot of the carved wooden bed, transformed into a dark, commanding *Dom* just by the sheer virtue of his intimidating stance, imposing presence, and a hard, virile body that exuded power, control, and authority.

Her mouth went dry and her knees went weak as she took in the total package. He was shirtless, and the form-fitting black leather pants he wore reinforced the image of a man in charge of tonight's play. The soft, lambskin material molded to his lean hips and muscular thighs, and instead of a zipper, the crotch of those pants laced up with leather ties for easy access.

But it was what he held in his hand that captured her full attention . . . the same leather crop she'd used on him last night. He struck the tip against his palm, and she literally jumped in place at the thought of that strip of leather snapping against the same tender places she'd smacked on his body.

Oh, shit.

A perverse, mocking smile curved his sensual lips as he strolled toward her. The sconces on the wall cast a red glow throughout the room and illuminated his handsome features. Without a shirt on, the muscles along his abdomen rippled, and her pulse began to throb a heavy beat.

The crop made a hissing sound through the air as he slapped it against his leather-clad leg. "Does this crop make you nervous?" he asked as he slowly circled around her, making her entire body tense with the anticipation of what he might do next.

She lifted her chin a fraction, refusing to admit that she *was* a bit anxious. "No."

Stopping behind her, he leaned in close, until his chest touched the silk covering her back and his lips brushed the shell of her ear. "No . . . *what?*"

"Sir?" she guessed, remembering his preference for that title when they were role playing.

He moved to her side and nodded his approval. "This crop should make you *very* nervous. You never know when I might use it, or where." To prove his point, he snapped the leather tip against the back of her bare thigh.

She gasped, her body jerking in response as that sting of pleasure/pain traveled straight to her sex. "Wh . . . what was that for?" she asked, frowning at him.

He raised the crop and dragged the leather patch along the curve of her breast where the silk lapels of her robe overlapped then flicked it along her rigid nipple. "Are you questioning me?" he asked in a dangerously low voice that both unnerved and excited her.

She quickly shook her head before he could deliver another punishing swat in more tender places. "No, sir."

"Good girl," he murmured, and set the crop down on the night stand next to the bed. "You'll be relieved to know that I don't intend to use this crop tonight—not unless you give me a reason to have to punish you. I just wanted to be sure that you knew what it felt like against your bare, sensitive skin."

And now that she had first-hand knowledge, she wasn't about to give him an excuse to wield it again.

"I have much more pleasurable things in mind for the two of us. Go into the bathroom," he said, indicating the adjoining bathroom.

She wanted to ask why, but knew better than to question Dean. Knowing she'd find out his reasons soon enough, she did as he ordered and walked into the spacious bathroom with her husband joining her. The large shower stall to the left had been modernized and upgraded, with luxurious shower heads and a sitting bench. A new granite sink and counter tops had been installed, along with a long length of mirror that allowed anyone in the shower to see his or her reflection. Just like the playroom, the bathroom was sensual and very self-indulgent.

He stopped her in front of the vanity and stepped behind her. The closeness of his body radiated a smoldering heat, as did the gaze that met hers in the reflection in front of them. "Since you seem to have a fascination with all the mirrors you had installed, let's put them to good use."

She still didn't understand why he'd chosen the bathroom when the four-poster bed had a mirrored canopy and headboard that gave them many variations of viewing angles. "There are plenty of mirrors out in the playroom."

"True, but this one is much more up close and personal." He slid his hands around her waist and untied the knot of her sash. "I want to make sure you can see everything I'm about to do to you, and watch your own response. I don't want you to miss a thing."

She bit her lower lip as he pushed the robe

off her shoulders. The silky fabric slid down her arms and fell to the floor around her bare feet, leaving her completely nude and feeling strangely vulnerable and exposed—even though Dean had seen her naked hundreds of times before.

But this was different, standing in front of a mirror with her husband watching over her shoulder, his gaze taking in every inch of her unclothed body. She liked to think she was confident in her nudity, but when she was forced to really look at herself—like now— without the diversion of wearing sexy lingerie or dim lighting to hide her imperfections, those deep-seated insecurities about her less-than-flawless body ran rampant.

She was soft and curvy, with full breasts that had lost their "perk" a long time ago, but the moment his big, warm hands slid along her stomach, all her uncertainties fled. His seductive, reverent caress spoke volumes, as did the thick, leather-clad cock pressing against her bottom. There was no fabricating that kind of insatiable desire. Closing her eyes, she leaned back against him, succumbing to the pleasure of his touch as his hands skimmed their way upward, to her breasts.

He didn't let her hide long. He gathered her breasts in his palms, squeezing both mounds as he whispered in her ear, "Open your eyes, Jillian." He waited until her lashes fluttered open and their gazes connected in the mirror before continuing. "Just look at you. You are so fucking beautiful."

His raw language, his honest declaration, made her melt.

"You have the softest lips." He nuzzled her cheek, his breath hot and damp against her skin. "And the prettiest, most irresistible mouth that knows exactly how to drive me crazy with wanting you. I love the way you kiss me, and especially the way you suck my cock."

His explicit words painted vivid images in her mind, and a moan of need escaped her throat as he continued seducing her senses.

"You have such great tits," he praised huskily as he stroked and massaged her breasts. "I love the way they sway and bounce when I'm fucking you. It's hot as hell and makes me so goddamn hard."

Oh, wow, she hadn't known that.

"Your nipples are so responsive, so sensi-tive. They're like hard cherries, so plump and sweet to suck." He rolled those taut buds between his long fingers then tugged hard on the stiffened tips, causing that twinge of pain to arrow straight down to her clitoris.

She gasped, both shocked and excited by the throbbing sensation gathering between her thighs.

He chuckled knowingly, the sound low and wicked as he continued to tweak her nipples, supplying another electrifying jolt of pleasure to her sex. "You like when I pinch your nipples, don't you?"

She nodded, unable to lie. "*Yes.*"

"I should have bought some nipple clamps today, too, but we'll save those for another time."

Ahhh, something new and erotic to look forward to.

He released her breasts and splayed his hands on her upper thighs. His thumbs grazed her smooth, waxed pussy then pressed steadily upward and inward. Those two fingers slid along the slick, inner lips of her sex, teasing and tormenting her.

He exhaled a long, slow gust of breath along her neck. "We haven't even talked about how much I love your cunt," he murmured, the sound of his voice filled with unbridled hunger as he penetrated her with two long fingers and used his thumb to rub her burgeoning clit. "You're so tight and hot, so creamy, and when I'm buried deep inside you, it's like I've died and gone to heaven."

She shuddered in need. Tossing her head back against his shoulder, she pushed her hips against the fingers fucking her, desperate for at least one of the orgasms he'd promised her earlier. "Dean, please, make me come."

"I'm getting there, baby girl. I promise." To her disappointment, he removed his fingers from her body then grabbed her wrists and pressed her palms against the cool granite surface in front of them. "Arch your back, and keep your hands flat on the counter."

She did as he ordered, her head automatically dropping forward, her eyes closing once again.

"*No.*" He slid his hand through her hair, gripping the strands tight to pull her head back and force her to look at her wanton reflection

—her body bent over, breasts heavy and full, and hips pushed back in a fuck-me position.

"Do *not* look away," he commanded in a deep, dark voice as he released her hair and caressed his hand down her spine and over the curve of her bottom. "Not unless you want to feel the sting of that crop against your ass a dozen times."

She swallowed hard, watching as he opened one of the vanity drawers and pulled out a tube of lubrication and what appeared to be an odd-shaped vibrator-type toy that was short, but smooth and curvy, with a flared end—and a small remote. Items he must have stashed there before she'd come down to the playroom.

He wedged a knee between her thighs, nudging them apart. "Spread your legs for me. I have more pleasurable plans in mind for that sweet ass of yours. Something I've been dying to do for a very long time."

She suddenly understood exactly what that toy was—an anal plug—and her stomach clenched at the thought of that toy invading such a forbidden place. As instructed, she widened her stance, and his right hand returned between her legs, his fingers lightly fondling her pussy. With his free hand, he picked up the toy, pressed a button on the remote, and the gadget buzzed to life. Slowly, leisurely, he ran the pulsating tip down her spine, increasing her anticipation of what was to come. He followed the crease of her ass all the way down to meet the touch of his fingers.

The moment the vibrator made contact with her sensitive clit, she jerked hard and nearly came right then and there. It felt like a hundred tongues lashing at her, and Dean quickly moved the toy away before she could splinter apart. He dipped the toy inside her sheath, again and again, until she was panting and moaning and willing to do anything for the orgasm he held just beyond her reach.

"You know what I want, don't you, baby girl?" he growled against her ear as he set the vibrator on the vanity, turned it off then added a generous amount of lubrication to the silicone plug.

Oh, she knew *exactly* what he wanted to do with the toy . . . and she wasn't about to deny him that fantasy, even if it wasn't *her* thing. "Yes," she whispered.

"Relax and breathe," he instructed as he

pressed the well-lubricated plug against her anal opening, slowly at first then more firmly, giving her no choice but to accept the foreign object.

She moaned as the rounded head stretched and burned its way past the tight ring of flesh, until it was seated completely inside her. It filled her full, pleasantly so, and wasn't nearly as bad as she'd thought it would be. In fact, it was quite arousing.

"Oh, fuck me," he rasped in appreciation. "That is so goddamn hot." He lifted his gaze to meet hers in the mirror, his irises dark with lust as he pushed the plug deeper still. "As soon as you're ready, I want to take you here, just like this."

Oh, God. She could barely handle the plug—she couldn't imagine Dean's sizeable cock invading that snug entry.

He switched the remote back on, and the toy pulsated to life, stimulating nerve endings she didn't even know existed. Moving behind her, he pressed the heated length of his body to her backside, still wearing those leather pants she wished he'd strip off so she could feel the hard ridge of his erection inside her, too. He

ERIKA WILDE

gently encircled her neck with one hand to
hold her head up so that her face was right next
to his, while his other hand disappeared
between her legs again, stroking her sex,
reigniting her need with skillful expertise.

"Jesus, Jillian, *look at you.*"

She looked at her reflection, seeing herself
through Dean's eyes. Seeing herself as a beautiful woman, wild and provocative and
completely *his.* Her face was flushed with
desire, her lashes half-mast, and her lips were
parted to accommodate her ragged breathing
as his fingers and the vibrations of the toy
worked in tandem to escalate her climb toward
release. Her hair was a disheveled, sexy mess,
unbridled passion etched her expression, and
the way Dean touched her, possessed her,
wholly dominated her . . .

"You're fucking gorgeous," he growled
huskily, his lips grazing her cheek while his
fingers strummed her clit in a way that beckoned her body to climax. "Come for me, baby
girl. *Just like this . . .*"

His command catapulted her right over the
edge. Her entire body trembled then exploded
in a heated rush that ripped a helpless cry from

her throat. The orgasm was like a flame searing along a fuse, spreading electrical shocks of pleasure through every inch of her . . . until he finally switched off the vibrator, allowing the sensations to recede—though he left the plug in place.

She moaned, her knees going weak, and he caught her up in his arms and carried her back out into the playroom. He laid her down on the bed then left her to retrieve some things from the armoire. Returning with newly purchased restraints, he straddled her waist and buckled a soft leather cuff, lined in plush faux fur, around one of her wrists. He looped the attached chain around a sturdy wooden slat in the headboard then secured her other hand so that her arms were stretched above her head and there was no escaping the cuffs the way he'd maneuvered out of the velvet ropes she'd used to tie him down last night.

"Perfect," he muttered, and trailed his fingers down her arms, lightly tickling her skin, raising her awareness of him all over again.

He moved off the bed and gently rolled her

over so that she was on her stomach. "Get on your knees so your ass is up," he ordered.

She was still so boneless from her orgasm, and must have taken too long to do his bidding —which wasn't easy to do while being shackled. He smacked her ass, hard, and she gasped in shock as the plug jarred within her, reminding her of its presence—as if she could forget.

"*Now*," he said, his sharp tone holding just enough threat to make her scramble into position.

There were so many mirrors in the playroom, there was no avoiding her reflection— her upper body pressed to the mattress, her cheek against the cool silk sheet, arms pulled tightly above her head, and her butt raised high in the air. She should have been embarrassed, but the image of her in such a helpless, submissive pose for her husband both intrigued and aroused her. While in the bathroom she'd been reluctant to watch, now she couldn't look away. She wanted to witness every dominant, aggressive move he made, wanted to watch the way he claimed her in such a dark, primitive manner with her restrained solely for his pleasure.

He walked around to the foot of the bed. "Spread your knees wide apart."

This time she was quick to obey, parting her thighs so that she was bared to him, in a way she'd never been before. The mirrors enabled her to watch him, too—the way his eyes darkened and his jaw clenched as he looked his fill of her pink, glistening flesh, and his own fascination with that wicked object he'd inserted into her rear.

He pressed a button on the remote in his hand, and she moaned as the vibrating mechanism turned back on, tingling along her sex and stimulating another round of restless, maddening need.

He moved up onto the bed and knelt behind her, his hands quickly going to the ties securing the front of his leather pants and the bulge straining against the closure. "I had a few other things I wanted to do to you tonight, but my cock is about to burst and I have to get inside of you."

He sounded desperate, and just as eager as she was to feel him plunging deep inside of her,

filling that space that ached for him. His erection finally freed, he rubbed the head of his
cock along her slick folds before finally
pushing inside her, hard and fast and balls
deep.

She cried out, the sensation of being filled
in *both* places at once shocking her senses. It
was like taking two cocks at once—incredibly
erotic and overwhelming at the same time.

"*Oh, fuck*," he breathed, clearly just as
stunned by how much tighter she was, as well
as the tingling vibrations licking along his
shaft.

He gave her a moment to adjust to the dual
penetration, but not long. Grasping her hips,
his fingers digging into her flesh, he held her
firmly in place as he thrust into her—long and
slow at first then gradually harder, deeper,
rougher. His entire body bristled with tension,
and she instinctively pushed back against him,
trying to alleviate the pressure building
within her.

"That's it, baby girl," he said, his voice low
and strained and resonating with carnal
hunger. "Push your ass up against me and take
it deeper. Fuck yourself on my cock."

His explicit words, the raw and primitive demand, made her hotter, wetter, and she surged back into his driving thrusts, impaling herself on his shaft as he'd directed. Again and again. He twisted her hair around his fist, using the long strands like reins to guide her, to control her movements as he pounded into her. To give them both the leverage they needed to get as deep as possible.

The way Dean handled her was all about possession and compliance, a savage, primitive mating that stripped away every inhibition and truly put him in command. The escalating heat was immense as he undulated his groin against hers, as she ground her hips rhythmically against his to increase the friction between them.

She looked into the mirrors again, captivated by how magnificent Dean looked in his element . . . so aggressive and dominant. Taking what he wanted, yet making sure her pleasure was just as great as his. His skin was damp, the corded muscles in his neck and arms bunching and flexing with each powerful thrust. His expression was merciless and fierce, like a warrior, and his eyes were so dark they looked pitch-black as he glanced down and watched his thick, veined cock piston inside her.

The sight of Dean in the throes of lust, his own urgency increasing, combined with the vibrating plug and the feeling of being full to bursting, was all too much for Jillian to withstand. Straining against the bonds shackling her wrists, she bucked against his hips, and with a low, feral growl he drove so far inside her that her whole body shook with the impact, creating a firestorm of sensations that sent her reeling and her blood pounding through her veins.

She screamed his name as her entire being seemed to come apart at the seams, the ecstasy rippling through her so intense she nearly blacked out. She convulsed around his cock, and he pulled her tighter against him as he slammed into her one last time. His entire body arched, his hips jerking as he came long and hard and deep.

He groaned and collapsed along her back, pressing her completely into the mattress, his breath hot against her neck. Too weak and sated to move or protest, she buried her face against the silk sheet. His cock still pulsed inside her . . . or was that the toy still on vibrating mode?

She was so sensitive, everywhere, and the internal buzzing was no longer arousing, but rather annoying. "Turn off the damn remote, Dean."

He lifted his head from her shoulder and chuckled, groping for the device he'd tossed on the bed. "I was wondering why my cock was still twitching."

She laughed, too, and was grateful when the humming ceased. Dean rolled off her, unbuckled the wrist cuffs so her hands were free once again, then drew her into a spooning position. He draped an arm loosely around her waist and nuzzled his face against her neck.

"Thank you," he murmured, the humble words of gratitude surprising her.

"For what?"

"For walking into my office and announcing you wanted to spice up our sex lives," he said, and not easily for a man who didn't normally voice his feelings and emotions. "For being open minded and letting me have my way with you, like tonight."

She skimmed her fingers down his strong, hair-roughened arm, loving the contrast of his masculinity to her softer, more feminine traits. "Just to be fair, you've let me have my way with you, too," she teased.

"Not nearly as fun," he said grumpily, clearly not liking the role reversal.

She smiled to herself. "You just like having all the control in the playroom."

He braced his head on his hand so that he could peer down at her, a dark brow raised much too arrogantly. "You haven't complained. Not once."

"That's because I'm too afraid you'll gag me," she replied, deadpan.

He blinked, looking totally taken aback and concerned that he'd gone too far with his ball gag threat. "Seriously?"

"No," she assured him, and he visibly relaxed. She turned toward him and stroked her hand along his chest, the light texture of hair just enough for her liking. "I like you being all macho and aggressive and alpha-male. It's hot."

A devastatingly bad-boy grin canted his mouth, the same one he'd used to seduce her back in high school, but now she knew just how potent and compelling everything about Dean Noble truly was.

"Good, because now that you've coaxed the dominant beast out to play, he's not going anywhere any time soon."

Jillian wouldn't have it any other way.

DEAN'S FANTASY FULFILLED

*A*t nearly nine in the evening, Dean walked into the house, tugging his tie loose as he started toward the master bedroom to strip out of his power suit, and to find his wife.

It had been a long Friday at work, and an even longer week of late-night meetings and negotiations to lure a high-profile client to sign on with Noble and Associates' security team. But all the over-time at the office had been well worth it. Dean and his partner, Mac, had sealed the deal and now held a multi-million dollar contract to provide security for the president of a transnational corporation.

He should have been exhausted, but the

adrenaline rush of triumph had him on a natural high, and he knew it would be a while before the exhilaration ebbed enough for him to truly relax. Then again, he was more than willing to burn off some extra energy in the playroom with his wife . . .

"Jillian?" he called out.

"I'm in here," she replied, her voice leading him in the direction he'd been headed.

He strolled a few feet into their bedroom and came to an abrupt halt the moment his gaze landed on her. He'd expected to find Jillian in a pair of sweats or her pajamas, but instead she was wearing a dark pink, form-fitting dress he'd never seen before—and he *definitely* would have remembered a sexy outfit like this one.

The low, rounded neckline revealed a mouth-watering amount of cleavage, and the sheath-like design hugged her curves like a lover. The hem of the dress ended mid-thigh, and the five-inch stiletto heels, with multiple straps that wrapped around her ankles, elongated her legs and seared images of them wrapped tight around his hips as he thrust deep inside her . . . with those fuck-me shoes still on her feet.

She'd styled her hair in those soft, disheveled waves that he loved, making her look as though she'd just tumbled out of bed after a long, hard ride on his cock.

He exhaled a harsh breath that did nothing to ease the tight knot of need gathering in his belly, and lower. "Where are you going dressed like that?" His attempt at a casual tone came out as more of a demand.

"Now that you're done with negotiations, you and I are going out tonight." She flashed him an irresistible smile as she crossed the room in front of him on her way to the dresser, where she slipped an array of gold bangle bracelets on her arm. "You've been working late all week, and I want a fun night out."

Her sultry perfume billowed around him, the soft, seductive scent making him harder than he already was. "I'd rather stay home and fuck you in those stilettos you're wearing," he said, point-blank.

She laughed, the sound throaty and much too enticing. "Later. I promise. You have fifteen minutes to shower, change, and be ready to go, or I'm leaving without you."

Like hell she was. She wasn't going anywhere dressed like *that*, without him.

He took a quick shower, and because she'd put a time limit on him, he didn't bother to shave the slight stubble shadowing his jaw. He brushed his teeth, quickly dried his hair, and changed into a pair of black jeans and a black dress shirt. In less than ten minutes, he was back in the bedroom and good to go.

Jillian propped her hands on her hips and pouted at him. "That's *so* unfair."

He pushed his feet into a pair of black leather loafers. "What is?"

"It took me over an hour to get ready," she grumbled good-naturedly, "and you look drop-dead gorgeous in just a few minutes' time."

"Just one of the perks of being a low-maintenance kind of guy." Grinning, he closed the distance between them, slid an arm around her waist, and pulled her close so their bodies aligned in all the right places. "However, just for the record, your efforts haven't gone unnoticed. You look stunning and sexy as hell."

She twined her arms around his neck, her gaze warming at the compliment. "Thank you."

He dipped his head and placed a soft, suckling kiss on her exposed neck, and she shivered in response. "You look *so* sexy, I'd rather just have you all to myself tonight," he breathed into her ear as he skimmed a hand down to the short hem of her dress and teased the tips of his fingers along the inside of her thigh.

She moaned, but instead of melting into him as he'd expected, she pushed his hand away and stepped back out of his embrace. "Nice try, but you owe me a night out. I've been patient and understanding all week while you worked late at the office, and I deserve to be rewarded."

He could think of a dozen different ways to *reward* her, none of which required leaving this bedroom, but she was intent on getting her way, and honestly, there was little he could deny his wife.

"Okay, let's do this," he said indulgently, figuring the sooner she got all her restlessness out of her system, the sooner they'd be back home and he could have her soft and willing beneath him.

"Trust me; you're going to enjoy yourself tonight, too." Promises and a bit of excitement glimmered in her eyes as she grabbed his car keys from the dresser then sashayed toward the bedroom door. "Come on. Let's go. Oh, and I'm driving tonight," she tossed over her shoulder.

He followed after her while processing her announcement that *she* was going to be sitting in the driver's seat, literally and figuratively, he was beginning to realize. Clearly, Jillian had something planned, and the evening's events were already thought out. He was just along for the wild ride.

She'd only driven his Aston Martin a few times, and never with such purpose and exhilaration. He watched as she expertly navigated the road in the sleek sports car, with one hand on the wheel and the other on the gear shift. Her fingers wrapped around the wooden knob, and her thumb absently glided over the smooth, rounded top—and there was no doubt in his mind that she was deliberately evoking mental images of her stroking something more phallic.

He had to admit that Jillian looked smokin' *hot* driving his car, in a tight pink dress, five-inch heels, and her full breasts pushed up even more by the seat belt strap across her chest. Sitting in the low-slung leather seat had bunched the hem of her dress up high, and every time she shifted the gears the sleek muscles in her thighs flexed oh-so-temptingly.

There was a newfound confidence about her tonight, in the way she handled the vehicle and even in the way she'd handled *him*. The slight smile curving her lips hinted at secrets she'd yet to reveal, and it suddenly dawned on Dean that he had no idea where she was taking him so late on a Friday night.

"Care to let me know where we're going?" he asked.

She cast a quick, teasing glance his way. "It's a surprise."

He frowned, not liking her answer. "You know I don't like surprises." At least not ones that he couldn't anticipate or figure out ahead of time. He liked being prepared and ready, and not knowing what awaited him not only went against that rein of control he liked to maintain, but also left him feeling too uncertain and antsy.

"Trust me," she said. "You're going to like

this surprise, so stop sulking like a little boy who isn't getting his way, or I just might have to spank *you* for a change."

"I'd like to see you try," he said arrogantly.

She laughed, unfazed by his words, or tone. "Big, bad Dean. You are *so* scary," she said, clearly mocking him. Clearly unafraid of him or his threats.

The corner of his mouth twitched, but he refused to let her see him grin and ruin his big, bad reputation. So, instead, he settled back into his seat and waited *impatiently* to find out their final destination.

A relatively short time later, they were driving through San Diego's Gaslamp Quarter, and Jillian finally pulled up behind the few cars waiting to valet park at the Stingaree, an upscale, exclusive night-club. So *not* his thing.

The car's windows were rolled up, but he could hear the loud music pouring out of the entrance as people entered and exited the establishment. A long line of people stood alongside the building, waiting for a chance to get inside. Considering the late hour and the crowd, there was little chance they would make it *into* the club.

He was more relieved than disappointed.

"Jillian, the line to get in is a mile long," he pointed out, hoping to convince her to head back home instead of wasting time hanging around for the next few hours. "The only way we'd get in tonight is being on the guest list."

"Which we are," she said as she eased the car up one more spot and flashed him a bright, I-got-it-covered grin. "Raina made a phone call for me, and all we have to do is check in with the bouncer at the front door and we're in."

Damn. He frowned out the passenger-side window, trying not to let his defeat show.

She wriggled in her seat, and he glanced over to see what she was doing. He stared in confusion as she reached beneath the short hem of her dress and skimmed her panties down her legs and off—not an easy feat in such cramped quarters.

What the hell was she doing?

She dangled the hot pink lace thong in front of him. "Hold on to these for me, will you?" she asked, her tone much too nonchalant, as if she stripped her panties off in public all the time.

He was so stunned and thrown by the unexpected action that he was rendered momentarily speechless. When he didn't immediately reach for the scrap of fabric, she dropped it into his lap and pulled up another notch in line. A young man dressed in an attendant uniform jogged toward their car.

"You really should put those away before the valet opens the door," Jillian suggested, amusement in her voice.

He snatched up the panties and shoved them into his jeans' front pocket just seconds before the driver's-side door opened and the kid, who was right about the same age as his sons, offered Jillian a hand to help her out of the seat—and all Dean could think was *Jesus Christ, she isn't wearing any underwear and we're about to head into a crowded, rowdy night club!*

He quickly got out of the car and met up with Jillian as she headed up to the entrance. Sure enough, their names were on a guest list granting them access to the exclusive mezzanine level, and the bouncer unhooked the red rope and let them pass through.

Dean tried one last time to get his wife to change her mind, using the only excuse he had left. "Jillian, you know I don't like to dance."

"I know, and I don't expect you to," she said over her shoulder as they followed a club host up the stairs to the mezzanine level, and away from the massively crowded main lounge. "You're here to *watch*."

Watch *what*? Other than her ass—which was bare beneath that short dress—as they climbed the stairs to the second floor. She was being much too vague, and it was starting to unnerve him. "Jillian—"

They'd reached the mezzanine level, and she turned around, cutting him off before he could voice his concern. "This is where we part ways, and you enjoy the show." She gave him a little finger wave and strolled toward the bar, drawing the attention of too many men in the area.

He stared after Jillian, her words, and their meaning, slamming into him full force. He was here to watch *her*, and the *show* she was referring to was the fantasy he'd revealed to her a few weeks ago . . . *I've thought about taking you to a night club wearing something really sexy and watching you dance and flirt with other guys and turn them on, all the while knowing I'd ultimately be the one to bury myself deep inside your sweet cunt.*

Holy shit. She was really going to go through with it and bring to life a hot scenario he'd only played out in his mind. The *idea* definitely intrigued and turned him on . . . yet as she slid onto one of the vacant seats at the long bar and ordered a drink, and a cluster of men sitting at a nearby table ogled her like vultures eyeing fresh meat, Dean questioned his sanity for letting any of it actually happen.

Then again, Jillian had obviously put a lot of thought into tonight, and he wondered if flirting with another man gave her a secret thrill, too.

Willing to see how things played out, Dean headed to the opposite end of the bar and sat down on a stool that gave him a clear view of Jillian, because he didn't intend to let her out of his sight. The male bartender delivered her glass of white wine, while the server at his end of the bar poured Dean a shot of premium scotch.

It didn't take long for one of the guys, who'd been watching Jillian since the moment she'd

ERIKA WILDE

strolled across the room, to break away from his pack of friends and approach her at the bar. The blond-haired man came up beside Jillian, his own drink in hand, and started talking to her. Dean had never mastered the art of reading lips, and he was dying to know what the other man was saying that put a bemused smile on her face.

Dean shifted restlessly in his seat and exhaled a deep breath. The guy hitting on his wife was at least ten years younger than Jillian, but at thirty-six, she was still extremely beautiful, with youthful features and a *real* woman's body—and clearly the guy was appreciating her assets because his eyes kept straying to the full, soft breasts displayed by the low-cut neckline of her dress.

Jillian turned more fully toward her admirer and gracefully crossed her legs—*thank God!* They continued to chat, laugh, and flirt while Jillian finished her glass of wine. All harmless banter, until the blond Adonis boldly placed his hand on her bare thigh and leaned in close to say something in Jillian's ear and Dean nearly came unhinged.

She wasn't wearing any goddamn panties!

His fingers tightened around his glass of

244

Scotch and he forced himself to stay put, which took extreme effort. *Did the guy not see the fucking three-carat diamond on her ring finger?* The one Dean had given to her on their tenth anniversary to replace the thin gold band she'd worn since the day he'd married her at the tender age of eighteen. The Harry Winston bauble was damn hard to miss, considering it nearly blinded Dean from where he sat across the room. She'd done nothing to hide the wedding ring, so obviously the Adonis didn't give a shit that she was married.

The guy said something else then inclined his head toward the stairs that led down to the main lounge. Jillian nodded in agreement and slid off the wooden seat, allowing the guy to escort her to the dance floor. Dean quickly downed the last of his drink, tossed a twenty to the bartender, and followed the two of them at a discreet distance. By the time he reached the clear glass railing framing the mezzanine level, they were already down below, engulfed in the sea of people dancing to the pulsing beat of the music.

From the second level, he had a straight-on view of the two of them, and it was both arousing and agonizing to watch Jillian dance with another man. Her body moved fluidly, sensually. Her hips swayed, her head fell back, and she put her arms above her head and executed an erotic shimmy that made her partner's eyes glaze over with lust.

The Adonis reached for her, put his hands on her waist, and spun her around so that Jillian's backside tucked right up against his groin. He began dirty dancing with her, grinding his hips against her ass, and a red haze of fury filled Dean's vision. He prided himself on being calm and controlled. He wasn't a violent man, but at the moment he wanted to kill the other man for touching Jillian so intimately.

He'd had enough, seen enough. A possessive rage clamored inside him as he made his way down to the main lounge then onto the dance floor, pushing his way through the throng of party revelers to get to his wife. His angry reaction was stronger than he ever would have imagined, confirming the knowledge that he wasn't the kind of man who could *ever* share. Jillian was *his*, and only his. And always would be.

He reached the two of them and shoved the man away from Jillian, making the crowd part around them. "Get the fuck away from her," Dean yelled above the music.

The guy stumbled back a few steps then bristled and puffed his chest out when he saw Dean, prepping for a fight.

Dean was more than ready to swing a fist or two. His entire body was filled with a tension that badly needed a release. This close, Dean was bigger than the other guy, stronger than him, and trained to *kill* with his bare hands. Yeah, he definitely had the advantage.

"What the hell?" the Adonis shouted back irritably.

Jillian's eyes were wide and startled. "Dean—"

"She's with *me*," Dean growled menacingly and stepped in front of Jillian in an unmistakable territorial gesture.

Seeing the dark, murderous expression on Dean's face, and realizing he was no match for him in size and strength, the other man put his hands up in a truce-like gesture. "I swear I didn't know, man!"

Dean almost felt sorry for the other man,

except the Adonis had blatantly ignored the fact that Jillian was clearly spoken for. He grabbed Jillian's wrist and thrust her left hand up into the guy's face. "She's wearing a goddamn wedding ring, asshole," he pointed out furiously, knowing that his temper was on the verge of really exploding. "Are you fucking *blind?*"

By now, the people around them had stopped dancing and had become spectators. The Adonis's face had turned red in embarrassment. "Sorry, man," he said, his tone sincere. "Nothing happened."

Dean glared, his hand curling into a tight fist he wanted to plant against the guy's chiseled jaw. "Damn right nothing happened!"

Jillian tugged on his arm, trying to pull his attention away from the other man. "Dean, let's go," she said, the distress in her voice finally penetrating the fog of outrage clouding his brain.

A part of him acknowledged that he was being irrational, but the jealousy burning in his gut had turned him into a raving mad-man, and he absolutely *hated* the loss of control. Before security came to diffuse the situation and escort them out, Dean clasped Jillian's hand in his and pulled her toward the exit. Once they were outside, he handed his valet ticket to an attendant, and a few minutes later his car arrived.

Jillian remained quiet until they were secluded in the car and he was on the road back to their house. His hands wrapped tightly around the wheel, his knuckles nearly white from his unrelenting grip, and his jaw was clenched so hard his teeth were grinding. He couldn't remember ever feeling this angry, this hot-headed, this *possessive* of his wife.

He was undeniably infuriated, but he was also bristling with heat-fueled lust and desire, and those intense, conflicting emotions were wreaking havoc with his mind and body. Need sizzled over his skin, adding to his internal battle to claim Jillian, to brand her, to make certain there wasn't a question in her mind that she belonged to *him*.

"Dean, are you okay?" she asked, her tone hesitant and worried.

"No," he bit out. "I'm fucking *livid*."

Out of the corner of his eye he saw her wince. "I thought you wanted—"

"Do *not* say another fucking word," he bit out, and immediately felt bad for snapping at her. His foul mood wasn't Jillian's fault. He *knew* that. He'd openly shared tonight's fantasy with her, had told her how much it would turn him on to be a voyeur while she flirted with another man, knowing he'd be the one to fuck her later, but he'd never expected reality to be so agonizing to watch. Never anticipated the twist and slicing pain of fear to nearly shred him apart—because good God, what if she'd *liked* having another man's hands all over her and he suddenly wasn't enough?

The thought made him insane, and he couldn't get home fast enough to reclaim what was his, to dominate every inch of Jillian and make sure that it was *his* scent that was imprinted all over her, inside and out, by the time he was done with her.

The moment they stepped inside the house, Dean pushed her up against the nearest wall, pinning her there with the muscular strength of his body. Bracing his hands on either side of her head, she looked up at him, her gaze wary and uncertain in the darkened shadows, and he asked the one question he couldn't get out of his head, no matter how hard he tried.

"Did you like him touching you?" he asked, his voice a low, feral growl.

"Yes," she admitted, very hesitantly, but honestly. "It was different and fun, but I kept thinking about *you.*"

"What about me?" he demanded.

She licked her bottom lip, her gaze bright with excitement, making Dean realize that his barbaric attitude was actually turning her on.

"I kept thinking about how good it was going to feel when you finally fucked me like you promised," she whispered, seducing him with her words. "It made me so hot knowing you were watching, that you were probably hard and thinking of all the different ways you wanted to take me once you had me alone. Thinking of *you* made me wet, not him."

He groaned, silently relieved by her admission.

Thrusting his hand into her hair, he twisted the strands around his fingers and pulled her head back, so that her mouth was just inches below his. "You weren't wearing any panties," he said gruffly, still unable to believe she'd shucked them only seconds before they'd exited the car.

"That was just to make things more exciting."

He pushed his hand beneath the hem of her dress and lightly traced the swollen, saturated folds of her sex, just enough to tease and torment her. "The thought of him touching your cunt made me goddamn crazy," he muttered.

Her breathing deepened as he drew lazy circles around her clit. "I . . . I wouldn't have let that happen."

"Me, either," he said fiercely. "Why do you think I stopped things when I did?"

She laughed softly, huskily. "Yeah, um, about that, you acted like an uncivilized caveman."

"I don't give a shit. That's my right as your husband," he said, tightening his fingers in her hair and tugging on her scalp so hard that she gasped. "You're *mine*, Jillian."

She moaned helplessly. "Yes."

"Your body is *mine*," he said, and thrust two long fingers deep inside her.

She inhaled sharply, and her hips instinctively jerked forward. "Yes."

"Your orgasms are *mine*." He glided his thumb across her clitoris, adding just enough pressure and friction to make her tremble with a need only *he* knew how to appease.

Her eyes darkened with desire as she rolled her hips, seeking the release he was holding just out of her reach. "Yes."

He skimmed his lips up to her ear, his breath hot and damp against her skin. "I own you, Jillian. Heart and soul," he said harshly, not caring how possessive or barbaric he sounded.

"Always," she whispered, her reply heartfelt and true.

"I will fucking kill any man who dares to touch you without my permission." His tone was ruthless, his threat real. "You belong to me. Only me. Do you understand?"

She lifted a hand and touched his face, forcing him to look into her beautiful, honest eyes. "Yes, I'm yours, Dean. There's only ever been you. You're everything I've ever wanted or needed, in every way. There will never be another man who excites me as much as you do."

Incredibly humbled by her declaration, Dean took her mouth in a soul-deep, tongue-tangling kiss that professed just how much he adored her. That he'd never be able to get enough of her. He pumped his fingers deep inside her body and caressed that hard nub of flesh, stoking her internal fire until she was dripping and writhing against his hand with the need to come.

He gave her body what it craved. She splintered apart, and he swallowed her unraveling moan. Her thighs shook, and her internal muscles clenched tight and hot around his fingers as she climaxed.

When he was done extracting every last bit of her orgasm, she sagged against the wall, her knees buckling. Without hesitation, and proving he was the barbarian she'd accused him of being, he hoisted her over his shoulder caveman-style and carried her to their bedroom.

"Seriously, Dean?" she said, laughter in her voice as her upper body bounced against his back.

"Oh, you have no idea just how seriously

uncivilized I can be," he said, and swatted her ass, hard, eliciting a startled yelp from her.

Once they were in the bedroom, he set her back down on her feet and easily slipped into the role of aggressive alpha-male. He wasn't even close to branding her tonight, to claiming the body that was made for his pleasure. When he was done with her, she would be utterly and completely satiated and marked by him.

"Take off your dress, now, before I tear it off you," he ordered as he stripped off his own shirt then removed his shoes and socks. "I want everything off but your heels."

Heat and excitement flared in her eyes as she quickly got rid of her dress then her bra. She stood before him, gloriously naked, those stilettoes accentuating her long legs and making his dick pulse with lust.

"Sit on the bed and lay back, so your legs are dangling over the edge."

Jillian did exactly as he instructed, and he strolled over to her, drinking in the sight of her all spread out for his enjoyment, her face flushed a soft shade of pink. Her hair was disheveled around her head, and her plump breasts were full, her nipples tight. Her stomach was curved and soft, and her mound was still waxed and bare. He couldn't see in-between her legs, couldn't look his fill of her gorgeous pussy because her thighs were closed much too primly, and he rectified that problem immediately.

He pressed his hands to the knees bent over the edge of the mattress and shoved them wide apart, a little more roughly than he'd intended. She gasped in shock but didn't fight him, didn't try and deny Dean what he wanted. She stared at him so trustingly, and that need to possess her swirled inside of him once again. Fierce, dominant emotions rose to the surface, heating his blood and thickening his cock.

He slid his splayed palms up her thighs, spreading her legs even more, until she was completely, indecently exposed to his avid gaze. He inhaled her musky scent, and his nostrils flared as the drugging essence of her seeped into his pores. "This is *mine*, Jillian," he said, and moved in to claim what was his.

"Yes," she breathed, and gasped when he pressed his open mouth against her sex.

His tongue parted her folds, hot and assertive, and he feasted and sucked on her as if she were a sweet, succulent, juicy peach. She cried out, both of her hands gripping fistfuls of his hair while her hips jerked against his determined, single-minded assault to make her come.

It didn't take long. His mouth devoured and pillaged, his tongue hit all her hot spots, and her entire body arched and shuddered as he sent her careening straight into ecstasy. She screamed hoarsely as she rode the intense waves of her orgasm, while his cock pulsed painfully beneath the confinement of denim.

Before she had a chance to fully recover, he flipped her over onto her stomach, her five-inch heels on the floor making her the perfect height for him to fuck from behind—just how he wanted it. Primal and animalistic. He tore at the buttons on his jeans, finally freeing the massive length of his cock while Jillian widened her stance and arched her hips to accommodate him better.

He dragged the head of his cock along her drenched pussy, but didn't thrust into her. Instead, he daringly glided the slick, moist tip of his erection between the cheeks of her ass, all the way up to that forbidden place he'd yet to claim. He'd expected her to protest, or maybe redirect him back to that safety zone, but instead she pushed her bottom against him and looked over her shoulder, her gaze heavy-lidded as she surrendered her body to him.

"Do it, Dean," she said huskily. "Take me the way you want to, the way *I* want you to."

He released a heat-filled breath. Her permission was like a precious gift, the plea-sure of which was all for him. It was like taking her virginity all over again, and he was deter-mined to make this so good for her, too.

He dipped his fingers into her cunt, using the thick, creamy moisture to liberally coat the length of his cock and to ease his way inside her ass. Satisfied that she was well lubricated, he positioned the tip of his shaft and slowly, gradually pressed forward. He was much larger, much thicker, much longer than the anal plug he'd used on her, and he immediately felt her body's resistance as the broad crown breached her.

She stiffened and moaned, her fingers curling into the comforter beneath her.

"Relax, baby girl," he murmured as he smoothed a hand down the slope of her spine, gently petting her, soothing her. "Just breathe and don't fight it. I want this to be so good, for both of us."

Eventually, the tension in her eased, allowing him to continue. He pushed in slowly, with more restraint than he ever believed possible when he was dying to be buried to the hilt. Holding on to her hips, he advanced inch by inch, watching as she took *all of him*, until he was fully embedded inside her.

He groaned, low and deep. Oh, fuck. She felt so tight and hot gripping him. His balls ached, and his dick was so engorged and rigid he had to forcibly resist the urge to rut into her like a savage beast.

But this wasn't just about him, and he leaned over her back, aligning their bodies and nuzzling her neck to give her time to adjust to the burning sensation of fullness.

"You feel so fucking amazing," he whispered into her ear as he pried her hands from the bed covers. He stretched her arms above her head and entwined his fingers with hers, pinning her completely beneath the strength and weight of his body. "Are you ready for me to fuck you?"

She turned her head to the side, her lashes fluttering closed. "I'm . . . I'm not sure."

He kissed her cheek, her jaw, the corner of her mouth. "I'll go slow, baby girl," he promised in a too-strained voice, and unable to wait a second longer to claim her, he finally *moved*.

He rocked gently against her bottom, slowly withdrawing before sliding into her again. The next thrust was a little harder. The one after that harder, and deeper, still. Each flex of his hips wrung a louder groan from her throat, and eventually, gradually, she softened beneath him.

"Oh, God, Dean . . ." Unexpectedly, she lifted her ass against his groin and pushed back onto him. Moaning, she arched her neck while rolling her hips in a sweet little grinding motion that made his eyes roll back in his head and shattered his control.

Knowing he was close to coming, he released one of her hands and slid his fingers between her legs, manipulating her clit with just the right amount of pressure and friction to set her off again. She began chanting his name like a prayer, and he powered more firmly into her, increasing in speed and force.

As soon as her cries of pleasure rent the air he gave himself over to his own searing orgasm. He threw back his head and howled like a primal, mating wolf as he emptied himself inside her, satisfaction and pleasure pummeling his body.

Utterly wasted, he fell against her, his chest blanketing her back and his face buried in the crook of her neck.

"*Mine,*" he grunted for good measure, and felt her laugh beneath him.

THE DECISION

a short while later, Dean lay in bed with Jillian curled against his side, her head on his chest, an arm draped across his waist, and her legs tangled with his. Her breathing was deep and even, peaceful and content, and while his body and mind were exhausted after everything they'd done, he couldn't sleep.

He couldn't stop thinking about tonight, and how his incredible wife had so boldly fulfilled not just one of his fantasies, but two. But after watching her flirt with another man, he had to admit that some fantasies were better left to the imagination, rather than played out in reality. He was grateful that Jillian had been open-minded enough to give him what he'd said he wanted . . . but she was *his*. He loved her, adored her, and tonight's scene at the club solidified the fact that only *he* had the right to touch her. For him, that point was non-negotiable.

Damn, but he was a lucky man, and he was so pleased that Jillian had taken the initiative to add a bit of spice to their sex life. As a result, their marriage was stronger, their intimacy closer and deeper, and there was a level of trust between them that paved the way for something else he had in mind. Something that had always tempted him, but he'd never believed that Jillian would agree to.

Until now.

Their twentieth wedding anniversary was next month, and there was a very special present he wanted to give his wife . . . but it was also something that would test the bond they were forging, while pushing their erotic limits. It was a gift that would either intrigue Jillian and enhance their sexual bliss, or she'd flat-out refuse his proposition.

Either way, he'd respect her decision.

Read on for an excerpt from THE INVITATION, the next book in The Marriage Diaries Series

THE INVITATION EXCERPT

"*I* can't believe you're getting a drink with me instead of going home to your wife. Don't *even* tell me that there's trouble in paradise."

Dean grinned at his best friend, Brent "Mac" MacMillan, who sat on a bar stool beside him at a local joint they frequented after work to relax and unwind. Though, admittedly, ever since Jillian had shown up at Dean's office weeks ago and propositioned him with spicing up their sex lives, he'd spent a helluva lot more time at home with his wife, than hanging out with the guys.

"Trust me, the only reason I'm sitting here

with you instead of being at home with Jillian is because I have a huge favor to ask."

"Anything," Mac said sincerely. "Just ask and it's yours."

Dean knew he spoke the truth because they'd always had each other's backs. They'd met in the Navy and served in the same SEAL platoon and were now business partners at Noble and Associates, the security firm that Dean and Mac had established when they'd retired from the military a few years ago. The two of them had started the company doing oddball security gigs, but with their training and experience they'd quickly become a prominent, multi-million dollar firm specializing in executive protection and corporate threat management.

Becoming a successful, viable corporation had taken a lot of time and dedication on both their parts, but all the blood, sweat, and leaner times had been well worth the sacrifice. Dean couldn't imagine any other partner than Mac. He was the brother Dean never had, and the one person he trusted implicitly.

Dean took a drink from his bottle of beer before getting to the point of the conversation. "Remember a few years ago when you asked if I was interested in an invitation to The Players Club?" The Players Club, a huge, massive estate located outside of San Diego in the hills of Fallbrook, was an exclusive, members-only society that catered to the erotic and forbidden. The only way to get inside the private, elite mansion was by invitation only by a current member, which Mac was.

"Yeah, I remember," Mac replied, a hint of curiosity tingeing his drawl. "And I distinctly recall you turning down the offer saying it wasn't Jillian's thing. Has that changed?"

"Possibly." He'd never brought up the subject of The Players Club to his wife, but considering how open-minded Jillian had become, he figured it was a good time to introduce yet another fantasy he'd entertained for years. And with their twentieth anniversary coming up, it seemed like the perfect gift, for the both of them.

Mac studied Dean for a moment before realization dawned. "Does this have anything to do with that day when Jillian dropped by your office, the two of you spent some time

ERIKA WILDE

alone, and she left with a big smile on her face and looking a bit disheveled?"

"Noticed that, did you?"

A knowing smirk curved the corner of Mac's lips. "Along with the fact that you couldn't concentrate on shit after she walked out."

Dean laughed, unable to deny his friend's claim. He had very fond memories of that day in his office—the day that changed so much between him and his wife, for the better. "Jillian has decided that with both the boys grown and out of the house, it's time to focus on us and making our sex life more interesting and daring."

"And how's that working out?" Mac asked before finishing off his beer.

"Fucking fantastic." Dean grinned. He wasn't one to share details, but he had to admit that even beyond the phenomenal sex, they'd become closer as a couple. Their relationship was more intimate, their interaction on a daily basis more fun and flirty.

"Lucky bastard," Mac muttered begrudgingly.

"What are you complaining about?" Dean

asked, amused by his friend's envious statement. "You always have some hot bombshell
ready and willing to warm your bed."

"Not the same thing." Mac sighed as he
absently wiped away the condensation on his
beer bottle with his fingers. "You're lucky
because your marriage has lasted nearly twenty
years and you still seem to be enjoying a
smokin' hot sex life. Do you know how rare
that is?"

Realizing which road they were suddenly
traveling, Dean grew serious. "You tried really
hard to make your marriage work, Mac. You
just rescued the wrong woman, and you never
should have married her."

Mac's lips thinned, as they always did
whenever they talked about the one woman
who'd ripped his heart out and stomped on it
for good measure. "I'm done rescuing. Period.
It's not worth the fucking hassle or emotional
turmoil."

Dean didn't argue, and just hoped that the
right woman came along to change Mac's mind
someday. But at the age of thirty-six, Mac was
set in his ways and certain he was better off a
bachelor who kept things simple and tempo-

rary. And being a member of The Players Club offered him easy, uncomplicated sex with a woman who enjoyed the same level of kink that he did.

"So, do you think Jillian is ready for a place like The Players Club?" Mac asked, effectively changing the subject off him and his failed marriage.

"I think she could be, yes," Dean replied. "She's become more adventurous lately, so I'd like to give her the option of accepting the invitation, or not, though I'm *not* interested in swinging or sharing." As he'd already learned that night she'd taken him to a night club, that point was absolutely non-negotiable.

"Trust me, there's something for everyone at The Players Club," Mac said, obviously speaking from his own personal experience. "And there are certain basic rules, and everyone abides by them or they're immediately banned. Nobody's going to touch Jillian."

"Not if they value their lives," Dean said, meaning it.

Mac chuckled and pushed his empty beer bottle across the bar. "Are you sure she'll be okay?" he asked, concern lacing his voice. "And

I'm not referring to just the sexual atmosphere, but the fact that she'll know people there. Like me, and a lot of our other guys."

Dean had already thought about that. "You've already assured me that there is a confidentiality clause in the contract that everyone signs, so I'm assuming that whatever happens at the club, stays at the club?"

Mac nodded. "Yes, and for those clients who don't know you, there are no last names exchanged to protect your privacy, as well."

Which was all very reassuring to Dean. "Then it's up to Jillian and how comfortable she is with everything." She would be the deciding factor, because he wasn't going to put his wife in situation that made her uneasy.

"Fair enough," Mac said in understanding. "I'll make a call and you should have the invitation in a few days."

"Perfect." Just in time for their twentieth anniversary. "I appreciate it."

Get THE INVITATION Now!

Other Books in
The Marriage Diaries Series

THE MARRIAGE DIARIES
THE INVITATION
THE CAPTURE

If you would like to know when my newest book will be released, please sign up for my newsletter here: www.erikawilde.com/social-newsletter-sign-up

ABOUT THE AUTHOR

To learn more about Erika Wilde and her upcoming releases, you can visit her at the following places on the web:

Website:

www.erikawilde.com

Facebook:

facebook.com/erikawildeauthorfanpage

Goodreads:

goodreads.com/erikawildeauthor

Printed in Great Britain
by Amazon